RETURN

_to_

NIMARA

THE REVENGE OF THE GWARKS

RETURN

to

NIMARA

Tanya Bourton

authorHOUSE®

AuthorHouse™ UK
1663 Liberty Drive
Bloomington, IN 47403 USA
www.authorhouse.co.uk
Phone: 0800.197.4150

Published by AuthorHouse 04/09/2015

ISBN: 978-1-5049-4060-3 (sc)
ISBN: 978-1-5049-4063-4 (e)

Print information available on the last page.

Book reviews from Amazon
Amazon reviews 5 star rating.

"This book is so well written. The descriptions are fantastic. Hard to put this book down as the author really has you wanting to find out what happens next. Excellent."

- Urszula

"The way the author describes the environments, events, and characters is fantastic. I was kept wanting to know what happened next right to the end. Hope there is more to come."

- M. Morris

"Wonderful read with great descriptive techniques which engage from beginning. Some fantastic insights to how our society is which really gets you thinking."

- Anne – Marie Golding

"Read the Plight of Nimara and found it thoroughly enjoyable. Kept you wanting to find out more and because of circumstances I read it in 2 sessions. The first 13 chapters in one go and then the rest of the book. The descriptions and scene settings are excellently described and not to verbose as tends to happen in some other books. I will not say too much about the book because it is well worth reading for yourself. Will certainly look forward to buying other books from this author."

- P. Mazzotta

For my wonderful Mother, Alicia.
You have always believed in me.

Contents

CHAPTER ONE

HOME

SUMMER KICKED OFF her sandals, flopped down onto her bed and stared up at the ceiling. Through the open window, the warm sunlight sent beams into her room and turned the floating dust into glittering specks that waltzed lazily in the air. It had been a beautiful June day and even though it was soon approaching the evening, it was still bright. Twisting her silky, long, blonde hair around her finger, she watched the floating specks hypnotically and let her mind drift to the day that she had just had. It had been a very busy day and even though she was excited, Summer felt nervous about the path that she was setting out for herself. Almost half way through her A-levels, she was ready to consider her next step. Without question it was always going to be University. Since the day she was born, her parents had set up a bank account where they placed whatever savings they had each month to be ready for when the time came.

'This money is not for a car or a house, Summer,' her father would look serious and speak in his booming voice. 'This is for when you go to University. Once you educate yourself the rest will fall into place.'

How many times had she heard that line, she thought to herself and smiled. At that time it all seemed so distant and unreal. Now, however, it was real and she had so many important decisions to make.

Summer had always wanted to work with children and was sure that she would make a fantastic Drama Teacher. This all changed after her experience on the planet of Nimara. Summer now felt destined to be a Science Teacher as she became fascinated by the wonderful things that the Nimarans could do.

Having researched University placements suitable for her, she had found so many interesting places to go; University of Central London, Liverpool, Newcastle and Edinburgh. Of course, she was grounded enough to know that Oxford or Cambridge was out of her reach. Wrapped up in the prospect of embarking on a new adventure caused her to almost forget one important factor, Bruno. All of these places were far away from home; far away from Bruno. Living in the small town of Cirencester was miles away from any of the places that she would inevitably go. Bristol was the nearest option, but with all the time she would have to dedicate to her studies, little time would be left for Bruno. Would their relationship cope with the strain of the distance between each other? Of course, she would not be actually going to University for another year and a half, but she was already considering the repercussions of her future.

Since finding each other again on Nimara, they were inseparable. They spent each waking hour together, sitting together at school and even their parents became good friends with each other. It was an unspoken expectation that they would be together for the rest of their lives. Of course, Summer loved him unconditionally and would not entertain the idea of being with anyone else, but a nagging doubt gnawed away at her thoughts. Did she have a strong enough faith in their relationship? Did she truly trust Bruno?

Closing her eyes she wanted to brush these negative ideas away and so allowed her mind to be swept to those of Nimara. How she missed that world and the people in it. Even though it was now two years ago, she could still remember the sights, smells and sounds of the planet. Her senses were so sensitive to it that she often believed that, in her dreams, she returned there. She could see the night sky which was velvet blue tinted with ribbons of deep red that waved like silk cloth, flapping in the cool air. The stars shone vibrantly and twinkled, reminding her of randomly scattered glitter. Each one appeared to be winking at her. The two suns and three moons shared the sky harmoniously so that the light spread equally across the horizon. She stopped and touched the many different flowers that nodded towards her, bopping with the gentle caress of the warm breeze. Each petal was smooth and cool to her touch and left exotic perfumes on her fingertips. The various smells, each beautiful on their own mixed to form a fragrance so sensational that Summer could not get enough of it. She breathed deeply, allowing her senses to become intoxicated.

A light tap at the window smashed her peaceful thoughts away like broken glass and she let out a sharp screech and jumped to the edge of the bed. She stared at the window from which the sound had come from.

A young man gazed down at her and laughed. His ginger hair was tousled, deliberately carved into a messy spiked up do, held in place by hair wax. He wore jeans and a plain white t-shirt which showed off his athletic physique. He perched precariously on the window sill, one arm firmly gripping the window frame above his head and the other holding the frame to the right of him. His arms, particularly in this position, made his muscles more pronounced and defined. Although nowhere near worthy of exceptional attention, his daily workouts had shown good results, gaining him a more masculine look than his age should allow.

'Hi gorgeous,' he called out to Summer and beamed broadly, 'How many times do I come through this way and it still makes you jump.' Smoothly, he jumped down to the floor and within a blink of an eye pulled her up, enclosed her in his arms and planted a gentle kiss on her lips.

Summer's mother shouted from below, 'Next time use the front door Bruno.'

'Yes Mrs Wilson,' Bruno called back respectfully then turned back to Summer and frowned, 'How does she know when I'm here? How does she do that?'

Giggling, Summer replied mockingly, 'You are not as light footed as you used to be, you've grown.'

'Are you saying I'm fat?' Bruno acted shocked and then teasingly tickled his girlfriend in the ribs.

Screaming, Summer tried to wriggle out of his grasp and playfully batted at his hands trying to swat them away. Finally, Bruno stopped and leaned in for a kiss. Summer held him close and kissed him tenderly. 'You shouldn't come in through the window really,' she pulled away from him and returned to her place at the edge of the bed. 'Firstly, it's dangerous, what if you slipped?'

'I have not slipped once in two years and am not about to now.' He grinned cheekily.

'Besides,' Summer continued, 'I might not have been properly dressed.'

Bruno was unsure of Summer's tone and his grin dropped into a frown. 'You've never worried about that before. How often have I seen you with your pink pyjamas and funky slippers?'

Summer stayed silent and looked up at Bruno. Slowly, her intense stare turned into resignation and her tense features melted into a softer, caring gaze. Dropping her head towards her lap, she watched her hands interlace nervously. 'I'm sorry. It's just been a difficult day. There is so much pressure to decide on Universities and courses.'

Bruno brightened up quickly and let his fears wash over him. Kneeling before Summer, he took her hands, unknotted them and then carefully wove each finger between his. 'Summer, nothing is going to break us up. Just because you have to go away for a little while, it will not stop me loving you. Besides, I will visit you and you will come home almost every weekend. We have absolutely nothing to worry about. Anyway, that's ages away, why think about it now?'

Summer lifted her eyes to meet his and the smile returned to her face. 'Yes, you are right, as usual.' She leaned her head on his shoulder, taking in the smell of his just washed hair and aftershave that he had started to use just a few months earlier. The St. Christopher that he wore brushed against her cheek.

'Remember it's my birthday in two days time.' Bruno's grip on her hands tightened with excitement.

This always made Summer laugh. No matter what age he was approaching, he never played it cool and maturely. She could imagine him as an old man, still acting like an excitable child when his birthday was close. Christmas was just the same too.

'Yes, I am fully aware that your Birthday is in two days time', she rolled her eyes and pretended to yawn from boredom. She then rolled off the next few sentences as though she had said it a million times before. 'I will come to your house for 10:30 in the morning and will give you your present as soon as I step through the door. I will wear the blue dress that you bought me for Christmas. I will stay all day and in the evening we will sneak out to spend some time by ourselves.'

'Is your Mum and Dad still coming?' Bruno asked eagerly.

'Of course they are. Have they ever missed your Birthday?' Summer cried in exasperation.

With that there was a knock at the door and Summer's mother slowly poked her head in. 'Is it safe?' she asked in a shy attempt to be funny. Her long hair was held in a tight bun and her shirt hung loosely, although still flattering her youthful figure. It was obvious where her daughter had got her looks and charm from. Bruno had grown to adore Mrs. Wilson for her patient and quiet demeanour. Nothing was ever too much trouble for her and she always had good things to say about people. She was a gentle woman who tolerated her husband's loud and brash sense of humour.

If opposites attract then there could not have been a better example of this than the Wilsons. She was attractive and radiant; he was getting bald and his shirts strained against his ever increasing waistline. As quiet and gentle as Summer's mother was, her father was loud and aggressive with his opinions. Mrs Wilson was often seen wincing at his jokes which were always inappropriate and ill timed. Mr Wilson constantly berated his wife for being too sensitive and easily hurt. However, they had a solid marriage and clearly were devoted to each other. Their relationship perplexed Bruno, yet made him hope for a lasting marriage like theirs one day.

'I have made chocolate chip cookies and they're fresh out of the oven.' Mrs Wilson gave her usual embarrassed smile and blushed unnecessarily.

The scent of home baked cookies filled the room. Without hesitation, Bruno bounded down the stairs in order to greedily consume as many as he could.

That evening, all four sat together in the conservatory eating far too many cookies and drinking. Mrs Wilson had a couple glasses of wine while her husband indulged in many bottles of beer. Bruno was allowed a bottle of beer while Summer joined her mother with a small glass of wine.

'So, Bruno,' Mr Wilson bellowed in his deep and growling voice. His face flushed with the heat of the day, 'How is the apprentice doing?'

Bruno immediately gave all his attention to Summer's father. He put down his glass on the side table and cleared his throat. Bruno knew that this was going to open up yet another uncomfortable conversation. Summer's parents were well respected members of the local community and were reasonably well off by anyone's standards. Mrs. Wilson was the Head of Department at the local Secondary school and Mr. Wilson was an established accountant; their expectations of people were high. Summer was destined for a career after University. On the other hand Bruno had chosen a less academic line. His father owned a car repairs shop in town and even though he would consider his business a success, he just about managed to pay the bills each month. He was not of the same status as Mr. Wilson. Mr Wilson owned a detached house in a quiet spot of Cirencester surrounded by trees and a little stream that ran past, weaving beneath a stone bridge. Bruno's father, Mr. Clement, owned a semi-detached house in a suburb just on the outskirts of the town centre. It faced a main road that was well used by those who wanted a short cut to the dual carriageway.

Bruno took a deep breath and forced a smile. Summer tensed up a little beside him while Mrs. Wilson lowered her head. She hated any kind of confrontation.

'It is going very well Mr. Wilson. My father said that I should pass all exams I need to be a car mechanic.' He paused waiting for a response.

'Good, good.' Mr Wilson replied, 'But, it's not exactly a career is it? What a young man like yourself should be aiming for is some kind of profession, for an example a doctor or lawyer.'

Bruno let out a brief, irritated giggle and replied with more determination, 'No it isn't. Not everyone can hold high positions. Everyone needs a mechanic at some point in their lives. Anyway, it keeps me happy and it's nice to work for my Dad.'

Summer placed her hand gently on Bruno's to re-assure him and gave him a loving smile. She liked the fact that Bruno had left school at sixteen in order to work in his dad's firm. The idea of her boyfriend, fixing heavy machinery and wearing overalls all day was a romantic one. It made him butch, more manly. She knew that many girls passed his garage and stopped to peer at him as he tinkled with things under the car bonnet, oil splashed up his arms.

'Well, it's lovely to see a young man eager to pay his way and work so hard. Bruno, you are a mature lad who knows what he wants. I admire that.' Mrs Wilson nodded and quickly flicked her eyes towards her husband. Bruno adored Summer's mother all the more for defying her husband in order to stand up for him. As always he could rely on her support.

Mr. Wilson sighed deeply and then took another sip of his beer. 'Well, good luck to you son. It's a hard job and doesn't pay well but you earn your keep and that's fair game to me.'

After this the conversation returned to more pleasant matters and laughter filled the room once more.

As Bruno started to walk home in the late evening he felt content. It had been a wonderful evening. Looking up at the cloudless night sky he thought about the distant planet that he missed so much and the people that he had grown so close to. His hand reached towards the St. Christopher around his neck and whispered, 'I wish you could have been here for my Birthday Granddad.' Tears started to form in his eyes and a lump began to rise in his throat. He missed Granddad more than anyone else.

It had been just over two years since he lost the man whom he met when the aliens had taken him. He had just turned fifteen and felt so grown up at the time. Looking back, he realised how naive and childish he had been. If he had not met and taken the advice given to him by Granddad, he was sure that he would never have been able to successfully lead the Nimaran army against The Gwarks. Besides, he could never take in the fact that Granddad had died sacrificing himself for him. Grandad had died to save him. If it was not for Granddad, Bruno would have been crushed under the weight of the bricks and mortar that cascaded down from the ceiling.

Only two years had passed, yet it felt like a lifetime ago. Bruno breathed deeply and wiped away the falling tears. Once again, like so many times before, he wished that he would one day return to Nimara.

CHAPTER TWO

ELZBIETA

THE NEXT DAY, Summer had a great deal to organise. She had decided to make a birthday cake for Bruno herself. The problem was she never baked a cake before and felt nervous in case it went horribly wrong. After a bit of thought she asked her mother for help. The tall, luxurious chocolate cake, hand piped with ribbons and a delicately written note of affection looked beautiful. Summer picked up the cake to put it into the dining room out of the kitchen. She accidently stumbled and the cake fell onto the floor. It looked like one big splodge.

Her mother tried to reassure her with a forced smile. The expression on her face clearly matched her horrified realisation that it was going to take some time to clear up the mess and start all over again.

'Mum!' Summer whined frustrated and left the room in a tantrum. She stormed up to her room and banged the door shut, leaving her mother in the kitchen to do the work.

Things were not going right and her next task was not going to be easy either. She had to contact Elzbieta. Summer liked and admired her a lot for the courage she showed during their time in the underground in Devon and for being the ultimate heroine in Nimara. Summer knew that she could never have taken the pill like Elzbieta had done and it was to prevent Bruno from having to take such a huge responsibility. The transformation back from alien form to human must have been excruciatingly painful and frightening. She could never have been certain that she would completely return back to her normal self. After all, the pill had never been tested on a human until then. Elzbieta never spoke of her experience to anyone. She kept it to herself. Summer was also very aware of Elzbieta's true feelings for Bruno, even though this too, had been kept hidden by silence. Elzbieta was a truly trustworthy friend and yet Summer could not help but feel threatened by her. 'Is it just jealousy?' She often pondered to herself even though she knew Bruno never had any intentions of leaving her for Elzbieta or anyone else for that matter.

Sighing to herself, she switched on her lap-top and looked at the time. It was 2pm, the time they had agreed to chat online. She connected with Elzbieta whose radiant smiling face filled the screen.

'Hi Summer, how are things?' She was full of joy to see her friend again.

'Good,' Summer replied, perking up a bit. It seemed strange to her that Elzbieta was always one step ahead of her in every way. Her hair had always looked fuller and longer than hers. She even developed quicker than her and already appeared to have a beautifully carved figure that would turn heads in the street. 'If she looks this good on screen what does she look like in the flesh now?' Summer muttered to herself. However, Elzbieta never felt that she was special at all. If she achieved something or did particularly well in anything she was amazed. She was not sure of her own abilities and this made her all the more wonderful.

'Hey, I have some news for you.' She beamed excitedly. Her sparkling blue eyes widened and her brilliant white teeth were fully visible. 'I have secured a place in Oxford. I passed my entrance exam for the University and got the A-level grades I needed. I've been dying to tell you for ages but I wanted to wait until we could speak face to face rather than by e-mail.'

Summer was sincerely happy for her friend but was not at all surprised by the news.

'Well done Elz, that's fantastic.'

Elzbieta, being a year older than Summer and Bruno was set to go to University in three months time.

'Elz, are you still able to come tomorrow for Bruno's Birthday?' Summer changed the subject.

'Of course I am. I have got everything organised. Is it still ok for me to stay over at your place? I know you and Bruno will want some time alone together after the party and I will go to bed.' Elzbieta said timidly.

Summer laughed as after all this time Elzbieta still was conscious of being in the way. 'It's fine, I will be so happy to see you again. It's been far too long.'

'Two years to be exact!' Elzbieta reminded her. 'Bruno still does not know that I am coming?'

Summer wanted to surprise Bruno and did not tell him about it. She knew that he would be ecstatic to see Elzbieta, their best friend from their adventure on Nimara.

'Just be at mine for 9am. We'll get you settled and make our way over to Bruno's for 10:30 ok?' Summer replied.

'Ok. See you tomorrow. It will be fantastic to see you both again. So much to talk about.' With that the screen went blank for a moment and was replaced with the words, Elzbieta has signed off.

Summer stared at the screen for a moment and thought to herself that yes, it would be fantastic for them to be together again.

Switching off her lap-top, she devoted some time to wrapping Bruno's present and signing a card for him. After this was done she went to her wardrobe and took out the blue dress that she would wear the next day. She remembered when Bruno had given her the dress at Christmas. She had been completely astounded as the dress was very expensive. On many occasions she had stopped at the shop window wishing that she could have it. The soft, thin fabric floated down to just above the model's legs and the whole dress fitted like a glove over the body. It was a strapless number fit for bright, hot days and Summer wanted it more than anything in the world and Bruno had bought it for her.

She placed the dress carefully back into the wardrobe and spun round towards the door. She had totally forgotten that she had left her poor mother in the kitchen. She dashed down the stairs and almost skidded on the tiled floor.

Her mother looked up at her as she entered and bashfully nodded towards the table. A sprinkle of icing sugar dusted her nose and her face was damp from hard work.

Summer followed her mother's nod towards the table and gasped. In the centre was the most magnificent cake that she had ever seen. It was a three tiered chocolate cake covered in shiny, smooth ganache. On the top was written in spiralling letters, Happy Birthday Bruno. It took a few moments for Summer to take it all in as she walked around the table to view it from all angles.

'Oh Mum!' she cried out in sheer adoration, 'It's just amazing, thank you.' She ran towards her mother who was smiling and gave her a huge hug. 'You are the best.'

CHAPTER THREE

BRUNO'S BIRTHDAY

THE SUN ROSE silently and peered through the gaps between the rows of houses; all of which stood like soldiers against the thin pavement that bordered the straight road. At this time of the morning, everything was still. Even the wind whispered gently along the path and combing through the short blades of grass that provided thin greenery against the edges of each house. A cat woke from its slumber, yawned, stretched then curled back up into a ball, letting its tail rock back and forth hypnotically.

Suddenly, in the distance a deep roar of an engine could be heard and a painful screech of tires grating against the tarmac beneath grew louder. It sped past so quickly that it was just a silver blur. It left a screen of black smoke that the old and inefficient exhaust puffed out continuously. Somewhere in the distance it screeched again and bellowed out a loud honk as the driver impatiently pressed on the horn.

Bruno's breath was heavy as he forced himself to open one eye. He hated that road so much. He rubbed his eyes with heavy hands and pulled himself out of the comfortable bed. He reached for the clock on the side table and brought it close towards his sleepy face in order to see the time. Seven o'clock in the morning. It was his Birthday. A smile appeared on his face and that soon became a toothy grin. He was now seventeen years old; almost an adult.

Bruno listened intently for any sound of activity in the house. To his disappointment there was none. It seemed as though his parents decided to stay in bed longer. Feeling a little hurt by the lack of any excitement, he got up and shuffled towards the bathroom. Little did he know, his parents were just at the bottom of the stairs, peering up at him as he crossed the landing. When he shut the door they stifled giggles and tip-toed into the kitchen in order to make the final preparations.

After washing he got dressed. He pulled on a pair of black jeans and put on an emerald shirt. This was his smart look. He smiled to himself as he remembered Summer telling him that she adored him in that shirt as the colour complimented his red hair. He looked in the mirror and stared at his reflection. The freckles on his nose still looked scattered carelessly and his eyes were a dark shade of brown. Many people told him that they looked warm and kind. He ruffled his hair into a messy style. In the morning light, his hair was a raging fire that glowed gloriously. Even through the shirt he could see his muscles were defined and this pleased him very much.

'No, I don't look any older than yesterday,' he laughed to himself and swung the bathroom door open, ready to start the day.

'Surprise!' his mum and dad screamed and pulled party poppers. The loud cracks of sound startled Bruno and a cascade of multi-coloured paper draped over his hair and shoulders.

'Come here honey; give your old mum a hug.' His mother pulled him close and cuddled him tightly. Bruno cuddled her back. He liked the fact that she was soft and warm as she had always been a plump woman. No matter how many diets she went on her weight stayed the same. This did not bother Bruno as he would not have changed her for the world.

He had always loved his mother but when he was taken away from her by the Nimarans, he vowed never to take her for granted. The pain of missing her was firmly etched in his memories and the fear of never to see her again still caused a lump in his throat and his eyes to glaze over with tears. He had learnt that time was precious and there was so little of it. One day, nature would cruelly separate them until it was his time to join her.

Bruno pulled away from his mother's firm grasp and looked at her. Her eyes were as brown as his and her gentle smile was as radiant as ever. Her hair was neatly cut into a short bob and was naturally straight. She wore her best dress that flowed modestly down to her calves and Bruno chuckled to himself as he realised that she was wearing the novelty slippers that he had bought her for Christmas. They were yellow and fluffy with two comically large eyes that danced around in plastic globes attempting to focus on who ever was looking at them.

'Don't forget me.' His dad grinned and reached out to pull him closer. Instead of a hug Bruno got a sharp pat on the back. Although loving and caring neither of them felt it was appropriate for men to embrace. Bruno may have inherited his mother's eyes but he looked like a copy of his father. He shared his red hair and dusting of freckles and was told on numerous occasions that his mannerisms were identical to his. Tall and muscular due to long days in the garage, his father looked good for his age.

Together they sat at the table and chatted about the day ahead and gorged on the breakfast feast that had been freshly prepared from six o'clock in the morning.

Time sped quickly and soon the doorbell rang. Bruno bounced up eagerly as he knew it would be Summer. He ran towards the door and opened it so quickly that it made the two young ladies on the other side jump.

Bruno's excited grin froze on his face as his eyes fixed upon the slender and beautiful girl who stood next to Summer.

'Elzbieta,' Bruno mouthed bewildered. After a brief pause he managed to compose himself. 'It has been too long. Wow, you look great!'

Summer flicked her eyes on Bruno and pouted slightly, however, she did not say a word.

'Wow, I mean…' he was lost for words.

'Happy Birthday Bruno,' Elzbieta smiled brightly.

Summer could not watch this little scene anymore and barged her way into the house. She called back to get their attention after leaving them on the doorstep,

'We brought you some presents.' Her voice was joyful and melodious but lurking just beneath was the sharp bite of jealousy.

Elzbieta looked at Bruno and raised her eyebrows in mock surprise and he returned the look with a sheepish lop sided smile. In an attempt to restore a more jovial atmosphere, he bowed dramatically, swiping his hand in the air and then nodded towards the open door to indicate that Elzbieta was invited into the house. Elzbieta chuckled at this and waltzed through the door.

Bruno led Elzbieta into the sitting room where Summer had already placed the presents on the table and sat comfortably on the pale green sofa. She patted the seat next to her and Bruno advanced towards her.

'You look amazing by the way.' Bruno winked and put his arm around her as he sank into his seat. This seemed to appease her as he could feel her whole body relax against him.

'Well, we have got homemade lemonade and biscuits. Lunch is at 12:30. Summer, what time did your parents say they will be coming?' Bruno's mother was a very bubbly host.

'They should be arriving at 12pm. My Dad had some work to finish off first.' Summer replied politely.

Bruno's mother responded thoughtfully, 'Yes, he does work so terribly hard. Well it is a responsible job being an accountant.'

'Mum is always snowed under mountains of paperwork these days.' Summer added eagerly.

'Now, I think it's time for Bruno to open up his presents!' Bruno's father interrupted.

This was followed by cheers and Bruno shifted position in order to be closer to the table. He looked at the labels and noticed the wide eyed expression of his parents as he read the one from them. The nervous excitement was evident as they clung to each other and bopped up and down.

Without hesitation he began to tear off the paper and was just about to see what was wrapped up inside …he disappeared.

There was a stunned silence.

Elzbieta and Summer exchanged a bewildered glance and slowly turned towards Bruno's parents. They stood like waxworks, perfectly still; clutching on to each other, their focus still remained where Bruno had just been ripping the paper off from his present.

Before the two girls could do any more they felt a strange sensation. The room began to blur and a sound like whooshing air was followed by the feeling of being sucked up into a black hole.

They too had disappeared.

CHAPTER FOUR

WELCOME BACK

BRUNO SAT AS still as a statue. His arms had remained extended, expecting to continue to shred through the wrapping paper that had been before him just seconds ago. With a vacant expression he stared transfixed at the empty space before him. Breathing heavily, he felt the quick and steady thump of his heart and the stabbing pain at his temples. Slowly, he lowered his arms and closed his gaping mouth. He scanned the room around him and saw that what replaced his comfortable, if not cluttered, sitting room was an empty space. He could not tell how spacious the room was due to the fact that everything was cream. No matter how hard he tried, he could not define where the floor ended and the walls began. The silence was eerie. He could hear his own breathing and nothing else. Then, it occurred to him that he could smell a strong odour that was clinical, like a dentist's room. A sudden thought caused his heart to beat faster and his eyes opened wide. An unsteady smile appeared on to his face at the idea that circled around in his head.

'It can't be...' Bruno whispered. The excitement bubbled clearly in his voice. 'After all this time, surely...' He continued to wrestle with his own mind.

Bruno knew full well that this could not be the underground hide-out that he had first been taken to even though the surroundings were very similar. He bowed his head at the terrible memories that haunted him since that horrific day. He could clearly hear the painful cries of those who failed to reach the door before the pit. He could see the look of panic as the metal door slid down, creating a barrier between the survivors and the victims. Worse of all he could not erase the image of Grandad, buried beneath the rubble that fell from the ceiling. He could still see his gentle, frail hand visible, showing off the wedding ring that glistened in the light.

Was it possible to be in Nimara considering it had taken three days by spaceship to get there? Confused but hopeful, Bruno continued to look around the room.

Bruno shot up from where he was sitting and raced towards where he thought the wall should end. Cautiously he slowed down and let his hands guide him until he touched the wall. It was warm and smooth with a texture that he could only recognise as belonging to the aliens. The material was definitely out of this world. Automatically, he removed his shoes and socks and let his bare feet brush against the floor. This too was warm and smooth, just like the walls.

His smile extended into an almighty grin and his cheeks flushed ferociously. 'Well?' he shouted out, 'Where are you?' He could not prevent himself from letting out a short chuckle and shook his head in bewilderment. 'I'm back!' he cried out.

A door swished open and an alien hovered gently into the room. Slowly he advanced towards Bruno and when he was within reaching distance he settled his feet to the floor and looked up at Bruno and smiled broadly.

Bruno was once again taken aback by the beauty of these creatures. He had forgotten just how amazing they were. Of course, he could never forget that their appearance in this form was far more sophisticated than the shoddy attempts in films and cartoons back on earth. However, it was the finer details that never ceased to leave him in awe. The thin, wiry neck barely supported the huge head that bobbed continuously due to the weight. The eyes that gazed into his were huge orbs of crystal that twinkled brightly; playing with the spectrum of light. They were intelligent, kind eyes that suggested trust and respect. When the alien blinked, the paper thin lids barely concealed the eyes. Although each feature was out of proportion, together it created the perfect structure.

The alien began to shake with excitement and tears welled in his eyes. Choked up he wailed 'Bruno!' and flung his arms out to the side and lunged forward to wrap them around Bruno's waist. His large head glued snugly against Bruno's stomach and he murmured, 'I missed you.'

'Charlie,' Bruno laughed joyously and peered down at the alien who was now grinning up at him. He had forgotten just how small and fragile the Nimarans were. 'I really missed you too.'

Charlie broke away from Bruno and tried to control the sheer delight in seeing his wonderful friend once more. Although he managed to compose himself to a certain degree, his foot tapped energetically which caused his body to quiver.

Both stared at each other and were lost for words. Their minds were so packed with questions to ask and stories to tell that they clogged up the ability to speak.

Finally, Bruno began, 'It's been two years Charlie. How are you? What have you been up to?'

'I'm fine, really,' Charlie replied and then paused. 'There is so much to catch up with and we must do so. Right now, Harry wants to see you.' Lowering his head solemnly caused a wave of panic to race through Bruno's whole body.

Bruno had already determined that Harry had not taken him away from his world for a social visit. There had to be a very serious reason for this. He dreaded to find out what it was and so hoped to put off the inevitable.

'How did I get here? I am still in my own clothes and it felt like barely a second had passed by. One minute I was opening my Birthday present then the next I'm here. It didn't happen like that last time.'

Charlie lifted his head proudly. 'It is a new system. I beamed you up.'

Bruno raised an eyebrow in jest. 'Beamed?' he questioned mockingly, 'Like in Star Trek? So, you interfered with my molecules and threw them across space?'

'No, nothing that inferior. It's in a way more simple than that but more difficult to explain.' Charlie clearly was in his element. 'I designed the whole system. It is a quicker way of transporting items from one place to another. You cease to be in one place and then you arrive at another. Let's just say, you disappear completely from one place then return in a different place.'

'You designed it?' Bruno was sincerely surprised. He knew that his little friend was adventurous and brave but did not know he was scientific too.

Charlie nodded, 'I am now chief engineer.'

Bruno patted Charlie on the shoulder and shook his head admiringly, 'That is so good to hear.' He was genuinely touched by the fact that Charlie was doing so well. He remembered what state he had left his friend after the battle against the Gwarks. Charlie had lost his whole family at the hands of the Gwarks and grieved bitterly. Bruno had seen the impact it had on the alien's personality which dwindled away almost to nothing. He was a lost soul caught in the tempestuous waves of despair and Bruno feared that he would drown. Yes, he admired Charlie greatly, more for his strength and courage than his ability to design spectacular machines.

'Follow me,' Charlie commanded, 'Harry is expecting you.' With this he turned sharply and quickly headed for the door. He glanced back at Bruno and grinned once more before leaving the room.

Bruno sighed and started to move towards the door too. 'Here we go again,' he muttered to himself, although inside he was ecstatic to be back.

CHAPTER FIVE

TWO YEARS OF PEACE

CHARLIE LED BRUNO through familiar corridors. The walls and floors were made of marble that, on closer inspection, formed an array of colours and shapes. The sconces burned brightly; its tongues of fire licked the air as they danced hypnotically. In the flickering light, the various colours glittered, twinkling and jumping along with shadows that swayed from side to side. Everything was alive in this world and seemed to celebrate Bruno's return. His feet made no sound on the floor, yet the silence was not sinister. It created an atmosphere so serene that Bruno felt all the nervous tension that had been piled on him back on Earth had been washed away. He felt calm, almost giddy by the release of every day burdens that furrowed his forehead and stiffened every muscle in his body. He too, felt more alive than he had every felt on Earth. This was what he missed about Nimara the most. Here, he felt free and that was the most euphoric feeling that could possibly be experienced by anyone, regardless of their age.

Walking with a noticeable skip, he followed Charlie, who from time to time turned to gaze up at Bruno with such delight that Bruno's heart melted. Occasionally, Charlie would point to rooms that Bruno was familiar with and his smile would become slightly melancholic as the memories were bitter sweet. Memories of a battle fought and won. Memories of lives saved and lost.

Through the many windows that he passed, Bruno could see the Nimaran people outside. Some sat on luxurious gold chairs that shimmered in the heat of the two suns. Others played beside the clear blue lake, its rhythmic movement caused by the pull of the three moons interrupted by the splashing of children. The elder members of the community played various card games and talked about a multitude of subjects whilst sipping on ice cold drinks. From time to time they stopped to watch the younger ones as they ran past, reminiscing over their own happy childhoods.

The birds in the sky sometimes swooped down to pick up crumbs that had spilled on the vibrant green grass. They were careful to avoid the babies that crawled towards them with hands that opened and shut in an attempt to catch them. The swans pirouetted in the lake and like the elder people, watched the young ones at play.

The scene was utopic and a sharp contrast to the serious faced soldiers who lined the pathways when he was last here. Everyone was at peace and the harmony between them all was truly beautiful.

Finally, Charlie stopped before a gigantic wooden door that was embellished with various gems of all sizes. The wood itself was rich and deep with a rose tinted shade of mahogany and highly polished. Charlie held up his hand and the door opened smoothly. He turned to Bruno and gestured for him to go in. Without a word, Bruno started to walk towards the door and as he past Charlie, he winked at him.

Once he crossed the threshold the door closed silently. Charlie had not followed him in. This room was similar to the one that Harry had used as an office in the underground hide-out on Earth. The furnishing was modest and functional. To Bruno's amusement the pencils in the pot were once again sharpened to a point and stood, unused like soldiers. The waste paper bin was empty and everything smelled new. Breathing in, Bruno could separate the various fragrances; the leather seats of the chairs that stood poised around a large wooden table, the varnish that had been carefully brushed on the table and even the lead of the upright pencils. Each smell was distinct but not overpowering, however, all were polished with the ever consistent disinfectant that was a theme throughout Nimara.

Behind the desk, just in front of Bruno, was Harry. His presence was as strong as ever and demanded respect. He leaned forward, hands placed lightly on the desk before him and he smiled. The round orbs of his eyes were moist with emotion yet he maintained a dignified, almost majestic stance. After a slight pause, he stood upright and then hovered round the table and stopped in front of Bruno. Slowly, Harry reached towards Bruno's face and gently patted him on the cheek. A tear slid down his face as he said, 'It has been too long my friend.' He breathed deeply to regain his composure and in a more formal tone commanded, 'Take a seat. We must talk.' He moved back towards his place behind the desk. Once settled into the seat of his large leather chair, he waited patiently for Bruno to do the same.

'You look older, more like a young man than a little boy now,' Harry said as he clasped his hands together on his lap. His frame was as small as ever which was emphasised by the sheer greatness of the chair. It seemed to engulf him in a protective cocoon.

'Well, I am seventeen today.' Bruno replied with an undertone of annoyance. 'I can't believe you took me away from my party. I was just about to open a present. Last time it was the day before my Birthday and so I missed it altogether. You have great timing!' Frowning, he pouted and glared at Harry.

Harry chuckled and sighed, 'Ah! still the child remains in the maturing body.' Shaking his head, he controlled his amusement at the expression on the boy's face. 'Mere coincidence Bruno, I do apologise. I can promise to return you to the exact moment when you were taken from earth this time. I am sure Charlie managed to explain about the advanced transporter that he created.'

'Yes, well a little bit,' Bruno admitted. He had already given in to the fact that his Birthday would have to wait for a while. 'But, what about my parents, Summer and Elzbieta? They surely could see that I disappeared.'

Harry raised his arm and with palm facing Bruno, gestured for him to stop talking. Even though Bruno had so many questions to ask he did stop. There was always no point in trying to control the conversation when Harry was involved. 'I will answer those questions all in good time. We have more serious things to discuss.'

Bruno shifted in his seat nervously, he did not like the word 'serious' to be used.

'You are probably wondering why, after all this time, I have brought you back to Nimara.' Harry looked at Bruno, it was clear that he was assessing how Bruno was reacting to the situation.

Bruno nodded but remained silent.

'For two whole years, we have had peace. We rebuilt our homes, our lives and strove to put the devastation caused by the Gwarks behind us. Of course, our hearts will never be truly mended but we must move forward as a people. We understand that to survive, we have to try and forgive. Turn to the next chapter in order to secure a better future. Take the experiences we have had (good or bad) and let it become a strength in us.' Harry stopped and lowered his eyes to the ground.

'I don't like where this is leading.' Bruno interrupted.

Harry flicked his eyelids up and stared straight into Bruno's eyes. 'To forgive and build a positive relationship with the Gwarks would have great benefits. We have strengths that they could learn from and they have theirs that would be good for us.'

Bruno could not digest what he was hearing, 'What? We fought against their army. They almost annihilated your whole planet and you want to forgive them? Are you totally insane?'

Choosing to ignore the outburst, Harry merely blinked at Bruno. He sighed and tried to explain himself again. 'Imagine if there was a way of creating an understanding between two people. They agree to cease battling against one other and share their strengths instead. Both would gain security and be better for what they have learnt from each other. I know it is too much to ask for to be friends, working side by side but at least tolerate each other.'

'What did you actually do?' Bruno barked frustrated by the naive attitude of the Nimaran race.

Harry leant back on his chair and prepared himself as he knew this would take some time. He also knew that it was important that Bruno knew and understood everything that had taken place.

'After you left, we had to rebuild our villages, towns and cities. So much had been lost and destroyed. Through hard work and determination we succeeded. However, we did not want anything like that to happen again. After numerous heated discussions with fellow politicians and a vote open to every person in Nimara, it was decided that to attempt to appease the Gwarks was the only way to prevent another war.

I was chosen to contact the leader of the Gwarks and put forward our request and what we could offer them. The Gwarks seemed to like the proposal and agreed not to attack again. I even shook the leader's hand as a sign of trust.' At this, Harry held his hands out to show them to Bruno. 'We promised to share our knowledge of medicine, environmental care and technical abilities.'

Bruno glowered at Harry, 'What do you mean by technical abilities?'

'Everything. We gave them our ability to transport people from anywhere in the universe to another place, our scientific advancements and weaponry.'

Bruno could not help but laugh at this. 'You gave the Gwarks everything that made you stronger than them. You helped them to be able to destroy you. I can't believe this.'

Harry knew that Bruno was right, 'They promised to help strengthen our army, protect us in times of need.'

'What happened to make you realise this was a total farce?'

It was now Harry who shifted in his seat nervously. 'We sent some of our top men to their planet with the instructions to teach them. The Gwarks tortured and killed them all. Worse of all, they sent a video link for us to watch what they did.' This last part of the sentence caused Harry's voice to break and he began to weep. He placed his hands on his large head and closed his eyes.

Bruno watched him sympathetically. He could not imagine how much it tortured this poor alien to know that he was, in part, responsible for more deaths.

'The Gwarks do not want peace,' Harry continued in sufferance, 'They want revenge. They feel humiliated by the fact that we won the fight. They are angry at the amount of men they lost. I fear that their anger has made them more dangerous.'

Bruno hesitatingly asked, 'how much did they learn from your top men before they killed them?'

The answer he got was what he feared, 'Enough to make a difference.'

At this Bruno's first burning question seemed irrelevant, but as promised, Harry gave him his answer. The only part that captured Bruno's attention was the fact that Summer and Elzbieta were also on Nimara. He needed them both now, more than ever.

CHAPTER SIX

IN MEMORY OF CARLOS

THE WARM BREEZE was sweet tempered as it caressed the cheeks of both Elzbieta and Summer. Sympathetically, the wind attempted to dry the tears that slowly ran down the contours and spilled off their chins. The impressive tree bowed down protectively, its branches swaying with the motion of the wind. At times, a leaf swept over the two blonde girls, reaching down to stroke their heads. Beneath the tree the flowers stood up, gazing towards the sky, eyes lifted to heaven in silent prayer. Their heavy heads bloomed with multi coloured petals that shone, wet with dew and their delicate, dark green leaves like arms outstretched vibrated slightly.

The two girls remained silent, isolated by their own mournful thoughts. They watched as the rows of candles, each one ablaze with flickering light fought against the kind air and remained as a constant reminder of all who died.

As soon as they arrived back in Nimara, Elzbieta felt compelled to return to this spot, although still dazed by the experience of returning. Summer followed reluctantly as her first thoughts were of Bruno and she wished to see him. However, the determined Elzbieta took control. Now, as they stood under the great tree, staring down at the plaque placed in tribute to Carlos, Summer realised that this was, in fact, where they both should be.

Ever since going back home, after the battle had been won, Elzbieta had lit candles in church and prayed for her dear friend, Carlos. She had not had any true friends before as it had always been just her mother and her. Carlos was the first person, besides her mother that she truly trusted. Of course she did have a thing for Bruno and in a way still did but this could never match the relationship that she had had with Carlos. She felt such deep guilt and shame. Guilt, as he had saved her life by giving his. The image of him stepping between her and the Gwarks to protect her was etched deeply in her mind. Seeing his anguished face as the laser burned a hole in his chest, the smell of cooked flesh, the light dying from his eyes pained her to the core. The moment he had reached out to clutch her hand as his soul began to depart from his body, he looked at her for the last time with adoration and love. She felt guilty as all too often she pushed him away instead of telling him how much his friendship meant to her. It was just her way, she did not like to show her true feelings to anyone except her mother. Now she regretted letting him die without knowing how much she cared. This gnawed away at her. This stopped her from building a close relationship with anyone else again.

Summer shifted closer to Elzbieta. She could clearly see the torment that the girl was going through but had no words worth saying. What could she say? Finally, she managed a quiet, 'He was so brave,' and left those words hanging in the air.

Bruno and Harry watched this tragic scene from a position at which they would not be noticed by the two girls. Bruno found it hard to stop himself from bursting into tears himself. He had been responsible for putting his three friends at the front of the line and knew full well that their fate was entirely in his own hands. He knew that Carlos was the weakest member of the group yet he failed to keep him safe. A decision had to be made, he knew that. However, he would often stay awake at night, wrecked with guilt at the idea that he had made the wrong decision.

Harry turned towards him and whispered, 'Carlos did what he felt was necessary. It was his decision alone.'

At this, Bruno turned his attention to Harry and managed a remorseful nod.

'Let's leave them alone for a while longer. I have something to show you.' Without any further explanation, Harry began to walk away and expected Bruno to follow.

Bruno once more glanced back at the two beautiful girls and then left them to their own thoughts and prayers. In the meantime, Harry already managed to walk quite a distance so Bruno had to run quickly to catch up with him and once more they walked side by side.

They walked into a garden that Bruno had not seen before. This area was at the back of the grand building. Two years ago he had entered via the front entrance after stepping off the spaceship. He had also left through the same entrance when going to and returning from battle. This time he was at the back of the building which led to fields of breath taking gardens. Nature was heavenly and here its work was in abundance. Trees of every height and width imaginable spread across the land, through which several rivers intertwined. Foaming with energy, the waves skipped over stones creating a bubbling symphony. Animals of every kind ran free, feeding off the thick carpet of grass. There were many varieties of wild flowers with a delicate fragrance that carried across to Bruno. Inhaling deeply, the fresh, exotic fumes cleared his senses and revitalised his mind.

Harry stopped and pointed. Following the length of his arm, Bruno noticed that at one corner of the garden was a small building. It was global in shape. The base of the building was made of white marble. Above this was a layer of gold encrusted crystals that twinkled in the light. The dome was made of stained glass of various colours and from where he was standing, Bruno could just make out that the patterns formed pictures. On top of the dome was a large cross, also gold. A winding path cut through the garden that led to the front door which was wide open, offering a warm invitation to anyone who may wish to enter.

'Is it a chapel?' Bruno asked. The beauty of the building was sensational. The open door spoke volumes of peace and sanctuary and caused a deep yearning in him to go inside. Without asking, Bruno half mesmerised stepped towards it. On closer inspection the chapel was dazzling. Its charm, boundless.

Harry watched as Bruno touched the doorway tenderly then vanished through the entrance.

Inside the chapel, Bruno was fascinated by the stream of colours that descended from the top of the dome through the stained windows. The room appeared to be far more spacious from the inside and full of light, though only a few candles were lit. Rows of seats were decorated with flowers that were perfectly arranged into small bouquets with deep blue silk ribbons wrapped around them. The floor was made of a light grey marble which led to a magnificent altar at the end of the room. Behind the altar, to Bruno's surprise, was a crucifix. The visage of Christ was gazing down with an expression of pure love. The whole atmosphere was one of peace. His attention turned to a statue that stood on a wooden table in the corner of the room next to a window that distinctly lit up. The light made it ethereal and Bruno was drawn towards it. The closer he got, the more his heart leapt in his chest. Even though the face was carved out of stone, it managed to capture the gentleness and kindness of the eyes of the beloved soul. The body was thin and frail yet stood proud. The hands that were clasped in front were delicate and thin. A wedding ring was clearly visible and Bruno reached towards it. As his fingers touched the stone, he fell forward and placed his head against the clasped hands. Tears run down Bruno's cheeks and he silently murmured, 'Granddad!'

Once he composed himself he looked at the plaque in front of the statue and smiled.

It read, 'Granddad, full of wisdom, love and courage that knew no limits. Let it shine forever in our hearts.'

This was indeed the perfect tribute for a perfect man.

Harry watched as Bruno emerged from the chapel. He felt sad yet content that the memory of Grandad would live on. Patiently, Harry let him take his time and merely regarded the boy with sympathy.

Bruno stopped right in front of Harry and took a deep breath, 'Thank you. Thank you so much.'

Harry raised his hand towards Bruno and stroked his cheek. 'Come on, we must talk with the other two.'

Side by side, the boy and the alien walked back towards the great building.

CHAPTER SEVEN

THE NEW ARRIVAL

BRUNO AND HARRY entered the kitchen to find Summer and Elzbieta sitting at the long oak table drinking hot chocolate. The marshmallows bobbed around on the surface of the dark, steaming liquid like bright pink and white balloons. The smell smacked him in the face and he breathed in deeply. The rich aroma was so pleasurable that instantly Bruno's stomach awoke and rumbled grimly, begging for a taste of the exquisite drink.

The two girls swung towards him as he entered and placing their mugs on the table, jumped up and ran towards him. Bruno winced at the high pitched squeals that threatened to perforate his eardrums as they expressed their joy of seeing him.

Summer opened her arms wide and wrapped them around Bruno. Laughing he lifted her off her feet and twirled her around. Elzbieta stopped a few paces behind and smiled gently as she watched them.

'Can you believe it? We are back. How amazing!' Summer spoke with excitement when Bruno dropped her gently back onto the floor.

'I know. It is good to be back.' Bruno returned, although his tone was less excitable than Summer's.

Elzbieta regarded him thoughtfully; she suspected that he already knew a lot more than they did. Of course she too realised that if the Nimarans brought them here, they had reason to do so. Inevitably, the reason was not going to be a happy one.

'Let's sit down shall we?' Harry's voice was clipped with authority and formality. He sat at the head of the table and placed his hands on top of it. Motionless he stared at the others and waited for them to take their places around the table.

Obediently, the three of them pulled out the chairs and sat down. Just as they settled down, Charlie emerged from behind the corner and put a mug of hot chocolate in front of Bruno. He smiled widely at him and then placed himself in the only vacant chair opposite Bruno.

'I would like to start by welcoming you all back to Nimara. Believe me, it is a great pleasure to see you all again.' Harry began, 'It amazes me how much you have changed in just two years.'

'You all look the same as you did back then.' Summer interrupted.

'Two years is not a long time when you are an adult.' Harry smiled back at Summer. 'However, a lot has happened in that time. After the battle, any survivors of the Gwarks went back to their world. They stayed quiet ever since. This allowed us the time to rebuild and move on. Most of our energy was spent on repairing the damage left by the Gwarks and believe me, there was much work to do.' Harry paused at this point and lowered his head. The devastation was still a black cloud that shadowed his thoughts.

The others sat in respectful silence and waited for him to speak again. Bruno blew on his hot chocolate while the others started to drink theirs. The marshmallows had melted and created a foaming pool that floated on the top of the chocolate.

'But, we were successful and are once again happy. In fact, a new sense of community has suddenly arisen. The people of Nimara fully understand the complexity and instability of their lives. What was once taken for granted is now deeply appreciated. Even the smallest of things have become monumentally important. There is a new found respect amongst the people and a great passion to live each day to the full. A sense of compassion has been extended to the Gwarks. If the peace and love that we share here could reach those who are unfortunate enough not to have experienced it, then our lives would be truly enriched and fulfilled.' Harry then looked at Bruno to see if he understood what they were trying to achieve by doing this.

Bruno just stared back at Harry, but the softness of his expression suggested that he did indeed understand. 'The bottom line is that the Gwarks used the situation for their own treacherous ends and now have the power to cause much more damage than previously. They now have the ammunition and worse of all the technical equipment including the transporter. We would not have any warning of their arrival.' Bruno said warily.

Harry admitted, 'This is true but I believe that they need some time to learn how to use them. They murdered our scientists before they learnt how to control the devices to their full potential. At least we have this much to our advantage.'

'So, what happens now?' Elzbieta was eager to know.

'That is what I wanted to get to,' Harry's pace quickened as he appeared to perk up. His large eyes shone with excitement. 'We must first get you settled into accommodation. Your stay will be longer than last time and so you will need more permanent bases. Summer and Elzbieta, my sister has been kind enough to offer to take you in to her home. She lives alone and so has two spare rooms. I think that you will find it very comfortable there. My sister is a kind and good humoured woman but I admit I am bias.' His smile radiated with pride and love.

The two girls looked at each other and then nodded their approval of this.

'Bruno,' Harry continued, 'You will stay at Charlie's apartment. It is very close to where my sister lives and so you will not be far away from the girls. I need you to keep the bond that you had last time. It was this bond that caused us to succeed in battle.'

Charlie sprung out of his chair and within a blink of an eye was standing next to Bruno, grinning excitedly.

'There is one more thing.' Harry became more serious, 'You will find that there is another person staying at Charlie's place. He will be an asset to you. You worked best in a group of four and so I took liberty of finding another fourth member for you.'

Elzbieta stood up sharply and opened her mouth to say something. Harry quickly prevented her from doing so.

'I do not in any way expect to ever replace Carlos. It would be foolish to even suggest that but please accept him and make him part of your group. It is this that I am depending on.'

Still standing, Summer was inquisitive, 'Well, who is he?'

'I will let him introduce himself when the time comes.'

CHAPTER EIGHT

A LOVELY PLACE TO STAY

AFTER HARRY LED out of the main building, he explained that they must walk through the gates of the city and continue in a straight line. A winding path would lead them to a small cottage. This was his sister's cottage and they would be welcomed.

As Summer and Elzbieta began their journey, they walked in silence as they both took in the magnificent sights around them. The last time they took this very road, it was barren. Of course, there were lots of fields surrounding them but the walk to the gate was short and unused. Now, by complete contrast, it was a hive of activity. The buzzing conversations of people as they sped to and fro were full of lively energy. Market stalls were packed high with an array of items tempting the passers-by. On one stall could be seen exotic fruits and vegetables that sat proudly, demanding to be admired. The colours were so vibrant and each item was a different shape and size. The natural growth of each fruit and vegetable was stunning and bewitched the two girls as they set eyes on them. On another stall, a variety of sweet smelling flowers adorned the tables that were set out for the purpose of their display. Some stood upright in pots, arms outstretched, observing the passers-by as they remained in their regal positions. Others bowed respectfully, offering their simple beauty, the eyes of their carpels lowered to the ground. Their leaves were brushing the pavement beneath; swaying in the breeze, desperately attempting to not be trodden on. From another stall, an alien bellowed out in his high pitched tone a language that neither Summer or Elzbieta could understand. When the aliens became excited their squeals became sharp and pierced painfully into the two girls' ears. When he stopped for a moment, the girls stopped wincing and saw that his stall was overflowing with pots full to the brim with scrumptious freshly made meals. Some bubbled thickly like molten lava whilst others evaporated steam that danced lazily into the air. The girls could smell the aroma from the stall that was blown towards them by the soft breeze with its intoxicating fragrances of spices and herbs. Swarms of aliens descended upon each stall, waving their money in the air and jumping up and down eager to buy the goods. Children laughed with delight and danced around with each other as the adults were being served. Jovial music could be heard coming from another direction and the children began to move to its beat.

The buildings that surrounded the central market square were enormous shards of ice that towered over like protective giants. Gleaming glass and metal bounced the rays of light, shining beams into the sky. With careful observation, it was obvious that a dynamic amount of activity was in progress inside each building. Lifts continuously rose and fell and aliens rushed past the windows. The city was thriving and very content.

The contrast between the medieval ambience of the market square and the futuristic architecture around it was intriguing. Just like everything else in Nimara, they worked together in harmony and made the whole city fascinating.

The two girls continued to walk and eventually found themselves at the foot of the large gateway. Here, everything was the same as the last time they were here. The metal walls still enclosed the entire city and the gates were just as massive and impressive as ever. Without warning the gate opened and lacking any sense of hesitation, the girls walked through it. They were now outside the city, excited to see what the cottage would be like.

'This must be the pathway.' Summer pointed to a bright orange path that was made from various shapes of stones. Although flat, there was no evidence of grouting and they had to tread carefully so as not to stumble in the cracks. Instead of annoying the two of them, this somehow made the journey even more enjoyable and adventurous. Giggling incessantly they moved precariously along the path.

The bushes and flowers that nodded at them as they past were familiar to fairy-tale settings. Even the wild life, curious of the intruders, stopped to stare at them before scurrying away. Along one side of the path, a river gushed down from a sheer drop making a magical display of spraying foam and droplets of water that poured down smoothly, before crashing on the ground beneath. Here, it rested in swirls before being pushed along, meandering towards the distance.

It was not long before the cottage was visible. Summer and Elzbieta broke into a run, eager to inspect the premises properly. Before the entrance to the building, there was a simple wooden gate that led to a garden filled with rows of ripened vegetables that poked out of the soil. Chickens ran after their chicks that were playing with the quails. A lamb skipped alongside her mother. The mother, bending her head down gently towards her child, stroked her tenderly. The cottage itself was also simple but beautiful. The chimney puffed out smoke that flew freely into the air. The walls were painted white and the door was open, ready to greet the new guests.

As the two girls past through the threshold they called out to see if anyone was home. They could smell homemade bread that was fresh out of the oven. As they ventured further inside they detected a new fragrance that made their mouths water. Fresh vegetable soup infused with rosemary and thyme. Searching for the source of the aromas and the noise of clanking spoons on pots and pans, they found themselves in the kitchen, watching a dainty looking alien slaving away at the stove. Steam twirled above a huge pot that was coated on one side with a thick layer of the soup that had spilled over. Inside the pot the soup simmered gently. Unaware of her audience the old woman mumbled to herself. Of course the girls did not know what she was saying but it was clear by her tone that she was frustrated with her baking progress. Suddenly she threw the ladle down into the pot and quickly turned around to gather something from the table. Seeing the girls, she threw her hands above her head in surprise and breathed in sharply. Then, she placed her hands down onto her heart and smiled sweetly at them.

'You must be the girls that Harry was sending to stay with me.' She rubbed her hands on her apron, then as an afterthought untied it and flung it down on a chair by the table. 'Please sit down, sit down, you must be exhausted from your travels.'

Elzbieta and Summer frowned at each other and Summer replied, 'It did not take us long to get here. In fact we rather enjoyed the walk.'

Moving the pan off the heat, the old alien gave a hearty laugh. 'Well I guess you are young. I find the walk more difficult these days. I imagine that Harry has not told you that I am his older sister?' she questioned them humorously. Then she continued, 'Please call me Rose. Harry made it clear that I had to pick a name for myself that you would be able to pronounce so, Rose it is. Do take a piece of cake. I made it specially this morning.' She took two plates out of the cupboard and placed them on the table. The girls stared in disbelief at the feast set before them.

The table was covered with plates of various breads and rolls with soft butter in a dish. A multitude of conserves were laid by the side of the butter. Three different cakes took centre place, an apple cake, chocolate cake and Victoria sponge generously filled with fresh cream and fruit.

'I always insist that my guests start with the sweet treats before the meal. It just makes everyone so much happier in my opinion.' She took a place at the table and began to slice the apple cake.

'I cannot help noticing that your home is not exactly in keeping with everything else in Nimara.' Elzbieta was careful not to offend the sweet lady.

'You mean old fashioned dear?' Rose replied enthusiastically. 'Yes, Harry knew I was curious about humans, especially after he told me about your heroic achievements here and so showed me pictures of life on your earth. I liked the idea of going back to simple pleasures and using my bare skills to cook and clean. I found it absolutely fascinating how primitive your ways are and decided I would give it a go. It is a hobby of mine at the moment and I must admit I am enjoying it.'

Summer and Elzbieta filled their mouths with cake and suspected that Rose had not entirely made it by hand. The flavour was intense and the texture was so light that it melted away before they could swallow. Instead of satisfying their hunger it caused them to crave for more.

Rose moved towards the soup pot and as she did Elzbieta spied bowls piled up in the sink. Some still held the remains of cake mixture. She caught Summer's attention by poking her arm and gestured towards the sink.

Summer mouthed, 'She really did make all this.' Her eyes glued to the food on the table, she gasped in amazement.

'Now for some soup and warm bread.' Rose's cheery voice was melodic and she picked up the heavy pot and waddled towards the table to find a place on which to put it down.

The soup was just as magnificent as the cake. The three of them began a lively conversation. Rose showed great interest in their lives as she did in feeding them.

At times she chuckled and clapped her hands, while at other times she gazed at them in astonishment. Summer and Elzbieta instantly took a liking to the old alien. They already felt at ease and knew that they would enjoy their stay in this cottage.

CHAPTER NINE

THE HEATED CONVERSATION

ELZBIETA HAD SURVEYED her room thoroughly; testing the bed, opening cupboards, rooting through the draws and perusing the books that lined the shelves. She was amazed to see that the clothes had been carefully arranged, folded or hung in specific areas of the room. Underwear was by the bed in the small storage box that served as a table. Casual attire took residence in the chest of draws that decorated one side of the room. A huge mirror hung on the wall above it. In the long and deep, fitted wardrobe, elegant dresses of various shades of blue, green, orange and yellow waited patiently to be admired. Each one had a pair of shoes to compliment the colour or style. Slowly, she ran her hands through the various fabrics and enjoyed the soft textures; silk, velvet, light cotton and many more. Each one promised to be comfortable to wear.

Her eyes were drawn to the huge, dark wooden chest that would not have looked out of place on a pirate's ship. She traipsed over to it and stroked the lid.

The wood was smooth and polished. She let her hands wander towards the golden clasp and lightly lifted it off the hook. It was not locked. She stood upright and paused. Biting her bottom lip she considered opening the chest. Obviously there could not be anything kept secret inside, otherwise Rose would not have carelessly left it unlocked. Besides, this was now her room for the duration of her stay.

Pouncing suddenly, she grabbed the sides of the lid and yanked it up quickly. Instead of treasure, the chest contained a great amount of paper. At first, Elzbieta was disappointed. Her mouth dropped down and she huffed, her excitement was gone. She was about to close the lid when she noticed a brightly coloured magazine cover that caught her attention. It was headlined, 'Human hero becomes one of us'. She stooped down for a closer inspection. The picture underneath the headline was of an alien charging forward. With teeth gritted and eyes full of venom, the alien looked satanic. Elzbieta's eyes widened and she could hardly breathe; the scene was all too familiar. This was the battle against the Gwarks and that alien was her.

She remembered all too well that the adrenaline rush was responsible for her quick decision to snatch the pill from Bruno and swallow it. She was reminded of the buzz she felt whilst soaring through the air and thrashing the Gwarks; Horror of losing Carlos to the clutches of death while trying to save her, so she could live. The physical pain she had to endure when changing back to her original form. Puzzled, she picked up the magazine and pondered on how this photograph of her could have been taken at that terrible time. The Nimarans never ceased to astonish her.

Sitting on the floor, she began to leaf through the entire magazine. Every article tracked the progress of their adventures. She relived the great memories that she held so close to her heart. It was a strange experience that was both pleasurable and painful. At times she giggled and at times she let the tears of sorrow pour down her cheeks. Everything was documented.

When she finished the magazine, she dropped it back into the chest and rummaged through the rest of the papers. Each piece was part of a huge collection of memorabilia paying homage to the humans who fought side by side with the Nimarans. Each piece praised them for their courage, determination and above all their strong bond that nothing could break.

Elzbieta thought about this deeply. Was their bond truly unbreakable? She thought back to the angry look Summer had given her when Bruno opened the door. She still felt the sting of Summer pushing past them and strutting angrily into the house, leaving her and Bruno on the doorstep.

She was fully aware of the fact that Summer was intensely jealous of her even though she tried so hard not to give her any reasons for this. She had stayed away from Bruno even though she was still strongly attracted to him. She had hoped that the time apart would slowly erase her emotions like the motion of the waves over grains of sand. However, the waves had merely covered them under shallow depths. On seeing Bruno again, the salt water pulled away to reveal the rawness of how she truly felt. Her sense of self pride bubbled with rage at the mere thought that Summer was over possessive and completely obsessed with Bruno. No-one was allowed to get close to him. She felt ashamed to admit to herself that often, she had wished, in fact hoped that Summer's erratic behaviour would choke and destroy the wonderful relationship she had with Bruno. She prayed that Bruno would wake up from the spell that Summer held over him. Just thinking about this caused Elzbieta's cheeks to burn. She was not proud of how she felt but she was unable to control her feelings.

Her attention returned to the wooden chest and she gently closed the lid. With her emotions still running high and the need to sort things out with Summer once and for all, with pursed lips she breathed deeply and stood up. Stiff with determination and hands clenched into fists, she left her room and paced towards Summer's.

She knocked loudly and without invitation opened the door and stepped inside. This room was very similar to her own but Summer had already managed to make it untidy. Various clothes lay crumpled on the bed and make up was scattered across the dresser drawer, many of which were left with the lids off. She could hear Summer humming a tune in the bathroom that led off from the main bedroom.

'Summer,' Elzbieta called, her tone was flat and hard. 'We need to talk.'

There was no reply and the humming continued.

Elzbieta moved towards the door and after a moment's hesitation reached for the handle and yanked the door open.

Summer screeched and turned quickly to see who the intruder was.

'Elz, did anyone teach you to knock first?' she cried out in a high pitched squeal. 'You made me jump.'

Elzbieta regarded Summer intensely and through gritted teeth muttered, 'I did knock but you couldn't hear me with the horrible din that you were making.'

Summer stepped out of the bathroom and slumped down onto the bed. She looked up at Elzbieta with an expression of concern. She had never seen her friend look so agitated before.

There was an awkward silence that thickened the atmosphere in the room.

With a deep sigh, Elzbieta abruptly chose to sit next to Summer and turned towards her.

'We really need to sort out a few things between us. I admit I have strong feelings for Bruno. I thought that had changed since we had not seen each other for so long but it hasn't.' Once the words started to flow she felt incapable of stopping them. 'But, you have got to get it into that thick skull of yours that I am not out to take him away from you. You are my friend, no matter how annoying you can be. We have been through so much together; more than anyone else on earth could ever experience. Anyway, Bruno loves you and always will. God knows why but he does. So get over it and stop acting like a spoilt brat.'

Summer gaped at Elzbieta stunned by her words. As she began to make sense of them she screamed out, 'How dare you burst into my bathroom and call me names.' She began to pant as her rage was now fully uncaged. Clawing back at Elzbieta, she growled, 'How dare you tell me about your feelings for Bruno!'

Elzbieta leapt up and backed away, her eyes wide with astonishment. She stared down at the beast before her and was at a loss for words.

Summer looked up at the girl who had grown pale. She raked her claws through her own hair savagely and rocked back and forth. Elzbieta remained transfixed by this and did not know what step to take next.

'Summer, I…' she began meekly hoping to calm the situation down.

This caused Summer to glare at her, the anger still unabated. 'Don't you dare speak to me like that. You are the one who is jealous. You are the spoilt brat. Carlos died because of you and you know that.'

Elzbieta flinched at what Summer had said to her. It was more hurtful than a punch in the face. Tears tumbled down her cheeks and she remained dumbfounded.

Slowly shaking her head she stuttered, 'You don't mean that. You don't mean that. I did not cause Carlos to die. He…we were in battle…he…' The tumbling tears became rivers of sorrow and regret. She fell to the floor and wept.

Summer watched this through a blurred vision and her hard expression softened. She knew that she had just spat out the wicked words and could not believe that she was capable of such a despicable thing.

'Elz, I'm sorry. I didn't mean it.' She whimpered quietly.

'It's what everyone thinks. Don't you think I think about it every day of my life? Yes, Carlos died because of me.' With these words she howled out in pain.

'I know that Bruno loves me.' Summer changed the line of conversation, 'It's just I cannot help the way I feel. I try; I really do try but…' Not able to complete her train of thoughts she left the sentence unfinished.

Again there was silence but this time it was for the two girls to make some sense of their outburst. The complexity and fragility of their lives at that moment was so intense, that it was too much for their youthful minds to grasp.

Elzbieta wiped her eyes.

'What now?' Summer asked.

Elzbieta smiled at this question that seemed so ridiculous yet so poignant and replied, 'We forgive each other and move on.'

'I really didn't mean to say what I did, you know that right?' Summer repeated.

'You meant it at the time but its ok,' replied Elzbieta. 'I meant what I said about not wanting to take Bruno from you, not that I could.'

'No, you would love to take Bruno from me,' said Summer. 'But I know it won't happen.'

'Stubborn as ever,' Elzbieta sighed but the atmosphere was much lighter and more friendly. 'You must come to my room; I have something to show you.'

Frowning, Summer followed Elzbieta.

Together they looked at the various magazines and news articles about their adventures in Nimara two years ago. At times they giggled and at times they grew serious, with the memories of what was gained and what was lost.

Quietly, knitting in her sitting room, comfortably moving with the rhythm of her old rocking chair, Rose listened and smiled to herself. Shaking her head slowly, she thought how good it was for the girls to sort out their problems.

CHAPTER TEN

CHARLIE'S HOME

As Summer and Elzbieta left to find Rose's house, Charlie led Bruno to his home which was closer to the edge of the city. Bruno was astonished by the hustle and bustle of the market square and often stopped to admire the fruits and vegetables displayed on the many tables. He too, marvelled at the variety of new buildings that had been built since the last time he had set foot in this place. It was hard to believe that not long ago, the whole planet was in danger of being totally destroyed and its people drained of all sense of hope, wallowing in despair and ruin. Now, the whole environment was alive with joy, thriving businesses and sense of pride at having achieved so much in such a short time.

'How did all this happen?' Bruno whispered to himself.

Charlie, who was bounding along beside him, impatiently waiting for Bruno to catch up with him, looked up at him and replied, 'With hard work and the need to repair what was lost.'

Seeing that Bruno did not quite understand his meaning, Charlie stopped and faced his friend and said, 'If we did not rebuild our land then the Gwarks would have succeeded in their quest to destroy us. All our brave warriors who fought so hard and lost their lives in doing so, would have done it for no purpose. We would have committed a great dishonour and ingratitude to their memory, therefore, we could not admit defeat. In order to commemorate those who had died, whether they were soldiers or not, we not only had to rebuild our planet, our lives and make things even better. We are proud of who we are and would not allow the Gwarks to win in any sense of the word; we won and improved.'

Looking around at the crowd of smiling faces, Bruno understood. These people were incredible.

Bruno's thoughts were interrupted by a sharp tug on his sleeve. Charlie was eager to move on. It made Bruno laugh to see just how excited Charlie was to show off his new home. Bruno remembered the sorrow and despair that Charlie went through when he found out that he lost his wife and two children at the hands of the foe. He now realised that Charlie's home was also destroyed and all the memories it held for him.

After Bruno and the others left Nimara to go home, Charlie returned to his to find it no longer existed. The garden was dug up with all the plants mashed by heavy boots and trees amputated. The stumps were a poor reminder of the tall and regal existences they once had. What once stood proud was crushed. The house itself was a crumbled mess of broken bricks and burning splinters. Nothing was identifiable as ash and bent metal skeletons made a graveyard of the ground. Was there no end to the poor alien's woes.

Harry welcomed Charlie into his own home and treated him with kindness at the time when he was most vulnerable. He waited patiently until Charlie gained strength to overcome the wounds of grief. Looking at the little alien now, as he exhumed energy and vitality, his passion to please and make his friend welcome was truly astounding. Here was a being to be admired.

It was not long before the two of them reached a high rise building made of metallic blue. Windows covered the structure from every side and sparkled in the light of the two suns. They entered through a sliding door that hissed as it opened and shut. A large foyer welcomed them and Bruno immediately noticed how minimalistic the décor was. The floor was silver and the walls a brilliant white. The front desk stood empty and so were the straight back chairs that lined the side of the wall. Although it lacked colour it was warm. Charlie led Bruno to the lift and pressed the button for floor 108.

The elevator was typical in size to the ones Bruno experienced back home but it moved more quickly yet smoothly. It took seconds to reach their floor without causing a sense of nausea. With a sharp ping, the doors slid open and instead of entering a corridor with many apartment doors, they stepped into a small room that served as an entranceway to Charlie's home. This too had brilliant white walls and a silver floor just like the one in the foyer.

Charlie skipped to the middle of the room, spun round, raised his hands in the air and proudly told his companion, 'Welcome to my home!' His eyes were wider than ever and shone with delight. The paper thin lids fluttered up and down like butterfly wings.

'You own the whole of floor 108?' Bruno gasped in surprise.

'Yes.' Charlie answered in a matter of fact way. He held his hands clasped in front and then smiled broadly. 'Come on, I'll show you around.'

Bruno had to admit that he was now very curious to see what the apartment looked like. He was sure that it would be beyond his wildest imagination.

The first room that they entered was a sharp contrast to the entranceway. The walls were painted a deep red and the floor was made of rich oak. Each plank was lined up perfectly and varnished so that it reflected the light that shone through the large window. The room itself was huge yet with a small amount of furniture. The use of minimalism exaggerated the size of the room even more due to the amount of empty spaces.

In the centre of the room was a crescent shaped sofa filled with plump cushions. Both the sofa and cushions appeared to be made out of soft velvet and was as red as the walls. In front of the sofa was a glass table that was empty. Bruno could imagine Charlie curling up comfortably on the sofa and reading a book or watching his favourite film whilst eating snacks from the table.

As if to confirm this idea, a thin, black, rectangular sheet hung on the wall opposite the sofa. When Charlie noticed Bruno staring at the sheet, he grinned mischievously and clicked his fingers. This switched the black rectangle on and filled the screen with fields of flowers and creatures similar to mice that scuttled across, searching for food. Bruno found it funny that this was the alien equivalent to a nature programme.

The sound was as crystal clear as the picture and Bruno found himself totally engrossed with the image before him. With another snap of the fingers and the screen returned to black silence.

On the walls were pictures of Charlie and his family. In one, all three stood together, posing for the photo. In another Charlie and his wife were holding a tiny alien baby wrapped in a pale blue blanket. Obviously this was the first photo of the new arrival to the family. On another wall, a wedding photo of the loving couple celebrating their new life together.

Bruno turned to Charlie and saw that he was looking at the photographs too. His eyes, focused on tiny details that were so important to him but missed by anyone else. He gazed longingly at them as though lost in the memories of times they shared together. These photographs meant everything to him. He turned to Bruno and smiled ruefully, 'They may not be here but they still live here with me.'

Bruno understood what was meant by this and so nodded but said nothing. There was nothing that he could say.

Suddenly there was a loud, reedy noise that came from the next room and a noise like something heavy knocking against metal. Bruno arched his eyebrows and frowned. He believed that they were alone.

Charlie's face lit up as he swiftly turned his attention to the direction of the noise. He smirked cheekily and grabbing Bruno's arm with both hands he tugged him saying, 'I have been dying to show you my little friend.'

The next room was also extremely spacious but Bruno could not identify its function on first glance. It was darker in this room and warmer. In fact the temperature was tropic, damp and close. He could hear the sound of running water and could not believe his eyes when he saw the fountain in the corner of the room. It was more suited to a palatial garden than a room in a house. The floor was covered in soil and moss. Plants of various species grew across the walls and even curled themselves around the curtain rod. Everywhere Bruno looked it was green; dark green, light green and even florescent green. A palm tree tapped him on the shoulder as he walked further into the room and ivy brushed his face; the dew leaving a wet trail across his cheek.

The same sound was made again and it made him jump. Locating the source of the sound, Bruno moved closer for inspection. A cave as tall as he was took up a quarter of the room. Its mouth was black and metal rods formed a gate across its opening. He reached out and touched the top of the cave; it was cold. It felt more like metal than stone and Bruno knocked on it in order to identify its material. The moment his knuckles wrapped on the hard surface a deep clanking noise was followed by an irritated roar. The sound was not like any animal that Bruno had heard before. He jumped back as a long, green tail flicked at the bars, back and forth, creating more clanking as it raked each solid bar.

Seeing Bruno's alarmed face, Charlie giggled, 'Its ok. It's only Herbert.'

Another great roar sent Bruno running to where Charlie stood some feet away from the cave.

From this distance Bruno could see two black beady eyes that in the centre were bright orange as though blazing fire was trapped inside. Smoke puffed out of the large nostrils. Charlie moved towards the cave and touched one of the bars. This caused the gate to open. Leaning towards the beast inside, Charlie began to stroke its head. The beast breathed steadily and with half closed eyes lowered his head down to the floor as if relaxing and revelling in his master's attention. After a moment, the beast opened his mouth to reveal a bright red tongue and two rows of impressively sharp spear-like teeth. It begun to sing a melody and the sound was enchanting. Bruno stared transfixed as the tune wrapped up around his senses, hypnotising him. Higher and higher the notes rose in perfect pitch. The voice was angelic; sweet and smooth.

The beast moved out of the cave and took centre stage. Its heavy paws sunk into the soil and its tail wagged side to side happily. The smoke continued to drizzle out of its nose like grey mist. All of a sudden, it fluttered its huge wings that expanded from either side of its body. Each flap made a soft breeze that moved Bruno's hair slightly. It smelled like the air just after it rains, damp but not unpleasant. Both wings were magnificent as they captured every colour of the rainbow and glistened like silk.

Charlie patted its nose lightly and the beast obediently stopped singing. Calmly, it folded its wings and sat lazily on the floor.

Bruno was dumbfounded and continued to stare at the beast.

'This is Herbert, my dragon,' Charlie announced like a proud father.

Bruno shook his head disbelievingly and asked, 'Is it THE dragon? The one you wanted some time ago?'

Charlie lowered his head briefly then looked at the dragon with such affection. 'Yes, the one my wife wanted to get me as a surprise.'

Bruno knew that this was a delicate subject to be talking about. The day that his wife and children went to buy the dragon was the day that the Gwarks attacked. The town was some distance to the south of the city and if they had not ventured out that day, they would perhaps have still been alive today.

'You bought it?' Bruno asked delicately.

'No. To be honest I hated it. My beautiful wife and children died because of my stupid admiration of it. I could not bear to look at it again.' Charlie sighed thoughtfully, 'The locals in the city wanted to show me how much they cared about me and raised the money to buy a new home for me. With the leftover money they decided to buy me a pet. They felt it would make a great companion in my time of need.' Charlie began to stroke the dragon's head once more. 'Slowly, I grew to love him again and now I could not part with him. He is so loving and gentle.'

There was a long silence as both of them stared at the dragon who was now falling to sleep on the floor. Its tail moved from side to side slower and slower until it stopped altogether.

Suddenly, there was a sudden bang of the door and heavy stomping of feet. 'Hi Charlie, I'm home.' A cheerful, out of breath voice was followed by an excited chuckle.

'Ah Greg's back. Sounds like he is up to mischief as usual,' Charlie explained.

'Greg?' Bruno was inquisitive.

'Yes, you need to meet him. He is the new member of the group that Harry was on about. He is staying with me as well. It will be one wild boys' party!'

Somehow, Bruno did not think that meeting this 'Greg' would be quite as pleasant as Charlie hoped for. He had already set himself up to dislike him. They did not need a new member in the group.

CHAPTER ELEVEN

GREG

EVER SINCE JOINING mainstream education at Queenstone School Academy in London, Greg was faced with many new adventures. For one thing he had never experienced being away from his mother's side as she insisted on educating him at home. Although he loved his mother dearly and enjoyed their time together, he felt too sheltered and wanted to taste a bit of freedom. Prior to going to school he was genuinely happy. He was constantly smiling and running around energetically, full of curiosity for what each day would bring; but he felt there was so much more. In the mornings he would stand by the front gate and watch as the other children boarded the school bus. They would laugh together and talk together and even mess around before stepping on to the waiting vehicle. All he did was watch and wave. Most of the time the other children would ignore him but sometimes one or two would wave back and giggle amongst themselves.

Greg knew that he did not fit in with the other children; he was different.

When the bus became a speck in the distance, Greg would turn around and run back into the house where his mother would be waiting with open arms and a loving, broad grin. Being both an intelligent and perceptive boy, he knew that behind that huge grin there was sorrow in her eyes. They would always remain glazed with more serious thoughts. Greg had a finely tuned intuition when it came to emotions and he was acutely aware of what was circulating in his mother's troubled mind. She wanted to wrap him up in her arms and keep him away from what was potentially a very cruel world. A world that lacked the ability to accept differences, a people who would jeer and crush the gentle hearted. A people who, in their ignorance felt that they were more superior, even though they were not. At the age of eleven, however, things changed dramatically; Greg was to venture out into the unknown. He was going to join the other children on the new school bus that would take them to Secondary school.

His mother fussed around him, making sure his tie was straight and that his massive school bag contained everything that he could possibly need. He stood, facing himself in the mirror and regarded himself carefully. His brown hair was combed so that it fell on either side of his head framing his round face. His slanting eyes were larger than ever and the fear he felt was clearly visible. His enigmatic smile appeared forced as this was the one time that he did not feel so happy but a little frightened. His arms dangled by his side and trembled slightly. His whole body spoke in volumes about the various feelings that tumbled around in his stomach. He was afraid to leave the safety of his home and did not like how his mother gulped back the tears that made her voice quiver. He wanted to hold her tightly and assure her that everything would be fine. He was aware of the fact that he had Down's syndrome. His parents constantly reminded him that his condition was not going to block him from having a very fulfilling life. If he worked hard, he would be able to find a job and perhaps settle down with a lovely girl. He could achieve anything he wanted. Of course he knew this but did the rest of the world?

He looked once more at his over combed hair and quickly ran his fingers through in order to mess them up a little bit. Satisfied with the outcome he grabbed his bag and walked towards the front door.

'Oh honey, you messed up your hair.' His mother gasped and was just about to pick up the comb again.

'Mum, stop it please.' Greg pleaded and stared intently right into his mother's eyes as though daring her to challenge his decision.

She paused for a moment then chuckled sadly to herself, 'You are growing up too fast my sweetie. Come here and give your Mum a hug.'

Greg walked forward and grasped her tightly. On letting go of her, he stared once more at his beautiful mother. She was not old at all; in fact she was very young. She had met the boy of her dreams at school and became pregnant at the age of seventeen. This, of course, caused dispute from both families but the couple were in love and swore to make things work. It was during the antenatal screening which took place within thirteen weeks and six days of pregnancy that the condition was made known. Although worried, the two of them used this knowledge to research into it and with the support of both families were ready to welcome the new arrival into their home.

They say a baby changes your life and this bundle of joy certainly changed his parent's lives. They became a close unit and were inseparable. Theirs was a home of joy and love.

Greg ran out of the house and with every few steps pirouetted around to wave to his mother. Finally, he jumped onto the bus and faced the other children who had already taken their seats.

He found an empty one near the back and balancing carefully, as the bus had already started its journey, he fell heavily into it. The boy next to him turned to face him and smiled.

Greg's nerves started to dissipate and he relaxed. He was ready to face anything today.

CHAPTER TWELVE

GREG GOES TO NIMARA

IT WAS NOW the first of June and Greg could not believe how quickly his first year of school had passed by. Almost straight away he had made many friends mainly due to his quick wit and humour. He adored his Learning Support Classes as well as the regular ones, and revelled in the different activities for each day. Although he would never admit it to anyone, he had a huge crush on the Teacher Assistant that spent most of her days with him. She was gentle and kind with the patience of a saint. Her long, curly hair was often placed in a loose ponytail and she smelled of freshly cut flowers, similar to the ones that his mother placed in a vase on the dining room table.

It was during a Drama lesson with Mr. Malone that he was called to the Learning Support Unit. Feeling frustrated, as his group were next to perform, he grabbed his bag and stomped towards the door. As he left he heard the teacher reassure him that they would wait with his group until he had returned.

As he continued to stomp down the corridor he muttered to himself, 'Sir knows that I will never make it back to class in time.'

Suddenly he stopped. The long and narrow corridor seemed even longer than it did before. The green painted walls became a blur towards the end and appeared to bend unnaturally. A white light suddenly shot towards him and as it reached his face everything went dark. He felt as though he was being sucked up into a vacuum and was unable to prevent it. His breathing became laboured and his chest felt tight. A strange whirring noise echoed in his ears and became louder and louder until he felt he could not take anymore. Then, silence. Greg had reached Nimara.

*

Now, as he placed the keys on the kitchen table, he could hear voices in the other room. Charlie obviously had company. Since he came to Nimara, he had taken everything in his stride. At first, of course he was worried that his parents would be frantic about his disappearance but when the Harry assured him that it would be taken care of and everything would be fine, it made him feel a lot happier about it all. There was also something about these aliens that made him trust them. He also got to like Charlie a lot because he allowed him a great deal of freedom.

Excited, he took a large cake out of a paper bag and placed it carefully on the table next to the keys and put the dragon treats on the floor. He made sure this was safely tucked under the table so that no-one could trip over the huge sack.

'Charlie I'm home.' Greg called out and chuckled when he looked back at the gigantic cake that sat proudly on the table. He knew that Charlie adored this kind of sweet treat and chocolate orange sponge cake was his all time favourite.

He could just about hear Charlie tell someone that he had to meet him and this aroused his curiosity. Was the person he was about to meet the ginger hair boy that they showed him in the magazines? He was concerned that he was expected to make friends with this boy and that he never really trusted people with ginger hair. He imagined that he would be bad tempered and boisterous. However, the aliens seemed to feel very strongly about this boy, even to the point of deep admiration. Life had surprised him many times before so he decided to keep an open mind on the subject until he got to know him.

Taking the initiative, he raced towards the dragon's room from where the voices were coming from.

As he burst through the door, two sets of eyes swung towards him. Charlie clapped his hands and did a little skip and cried out, 'Greg, here you are.' Greg liked the fact that his friend was always so jubilant to see him.

Greg then turned to the ginger haired boy and his heart sunk immediately. The boy glared at him through narrow eyes and his lips were pursed together. He felt that he could have handled this but it was the next expression that stunned him. After a year of being liked and accepted for who he was, he had forgotten what it was like to be looked at disapprovingly due to his physical appearance.

The boy's face changed into a look of astonishment and disbelief. He gaped comically and gave a small huff of disapproval. He swiftly turned to Charlie and whilst pointing at Greg laughed, 'This is Greg?'

At this, Charlie smacked the palms of his hands on his own cheeks and looked up at the boy in panic. He paused, and then frowned as he could not understand this reaction to Greg's entrance. He swung his head to Greg and then back to the other boy and was at a loss of what to do or say next.

The atmosphere grew claustrophobic and even the dragon lifted an eyelid carefully. Feeling such an intense atmosphere, he decided to close his eye again and drift back to sleep.

After a long hesitation, Charlie announced, 'I think we better go and see Harry.'

CHAPTER THIRTEEN

THE DISAGREEMENT

HARRY SUNK DOWN into his chair and sighed heavily. Folding his arms, he stared intensely at the two boys before him. The silence in the room was a heavy, black cloud that threatened to suck the oxygen out of the boys' lungs. Uncomfortable and tense, they sat side by side, neither of them able to take more than shallow breaths. It was obvious that Harry was not happy with the way they had behaved earlier.

Charlie waited in the doorway as if ready to escape or at least become invisible in the shadow that darkened the corner of the room. He never felt comfortable during difficult circumstances; he lowered his eyes and fidgeted with his shirt.

After some time, Harry finally spoke and his tone was serious and slow. His enigmatic presence filled the room which demanded respect and undivided attention. 'I am displeased that you two seem to dislike one another,' he began. 'I cannot believe how your obsessions with each other's differences have caused such negative emotions. You both have such potential and yet are held back by the faults of humankind.' Slowly, he stood up and leaning forward, placed his hands gently on the desk. Again he regarded the two boys, first Bruno and then Greg. Shaking his head; he stood erect and knotting his hands in front of himself began to pace the room. Three pairs of eyes followed his every movement. Pausing to look out of the office window he spoke once more. 'Bruno, why are you so determined to dislike Greg?'

At the mention of his name, Bruno sat up straight. He gave Greg a quick glance as he did not want to expose his feelings in front of the other boy. It would hurt Greg, who did not deserve this and would embarrass Bruno to admit his prejudices.

Harry swung round and waited for an answer.

Bruno tried to find the right words, 'You know that Summer, Elzbieta and I have our friendship and it is strong. We lost Carlos who was part of that bond and no-one could replace him.' Again he looked at Greg who sat very still, mouth open in concentration and eyes full of hope and wonder. Averting his gaze, Bruno gave up fighting against the truth and admitted, 'It is a matter of life and death against the Gwarks. I don't think Greg could be any use to us as he suffers from a disability.' His cheeks became bright red and blood pulsed inside his head.

'I have Downs Syndrome. It is a condition not a disease.' Greg replied with sarcasm.

'Let me deal with this,' Harry ordered and his expression softened for the first time. 'So, you do not like Greg because he is different? I always was led to believe that differences are what make us interesting.

Would it not be a boring world if everyone was the same?'

'Yes I do agree with that but Greg could not fight against the Gwarks. Look at him.' Bruno had grown frustrated.

'And how do you know that he is unable to fight? Who are you to judge what someone can or cannot do? You have barely got to meet him let alone know him for his strengths.' Harry's impatience was obvious. 'Bruno, I have watched you grow as a person and witnessed your compassionate side but sometimes I believe that you have not progressed at all. You are still the immature, cocky little boy and that is your failing.'

Stunned, Bruno was speechless and gawped at Harry.

Greg gave a little snigger and smiled smugly. At this Harry turned his attention to him. 'Don't think that you will escape my anger. You are not a victim here. Stop being suspicious of others, especially because of something so ridiculous like the colour of their hair.'

Bruno whipped his head round and gave Greg an evil glare whilst Greg sat wide eyed, astonished that Harry could know his thoughts so well.

'Bruno, you know full well that you should trust my decisions. I take my responsibilities very seriously. Nimara and its people are the very core of my heart and you have earned your place in it too. Greg has qualities just like any one of us, his determination and willingness to succeed will be an iron fortress for you. You will see.' With this, Harry smiled and placed his hand on Bruno's shoulder. After a moment he released his grip and added, 'Summer and Elzbieta should be here in a moment. I have asked my sister Rose to bring them to me. I think you should all talk together.'

Just as these words were spoken there was a loud, enthusiastic voice chattering beyond the door. Someone was talking non-stop. Even though the words spoken were not clear the sound of intermittent laughter was. Harry's face was no longer serious and to Bruno's relief he broke into a huge grin.

Charlie responded to the sounds beyond the door and the weight of the atmosphere within the room was swept away. He jumped up enthusiastically and announced, 'They are here!' before moving away from the opening door.

As soon as the door swished open the sound of Rose's voice became instantly clearer.

'Well, as I always say, if you like that kind of thing then it is fine by me but I think it is just a waste of money!' Obviously she was in mid flow of a debate with herself and the two girls who had entered with her were merely an audience who listened politely but with much amusement. Once in the room Rose stopped babbling to herself and looked at her brother lovingly. 'Harry, I have brought them as you asked. It's about time we caught up with things as well. You are always so busy.'

'Thank you Rose and you know what it is like for me.' Harry moved towards her and gave her a gentle peck on the cheek.

Rose turned to the two girls and frowned, 'Ok, Ok so he may be the most important person in Nimara but he could still make time for his family.' She shifted her attention to Bruno and Greg, 'Ah so here you are, the rest of the group. I am so honoured to meet you Bruno and a pleasure to meet you Greg.'

Greg could not believe that this charming lady had not even blinked when she set eyes on him. Bruno became bashful at her respect for him. Both boys instantly became fond of her and could not supress eager expressions of delight when they gazed down at her.

Summer and Elzbieta moved towards Bruno and stared inquisitively at Greg. Seeing this, Harry told them, 'Bruno will introduce you; go out into the garden, I am sure you have much to talk about. Rose and I have some catching up to do ourselves.

At this the four young individuals left the room, full of conversations bursting to be told.

As soon as they were gone, Harry turned to his sister, 'Now let's go for a drink.'

'Ooh I could do with something a bit stronger than tea,' Rose smirked cheekily.

'I was anticipating that.' Harry responded full of humour.

Charlie watched as they too left the room and for a few moments remained standing alone. He was considering what to do with his spare time when a sharp tap at the window made him jump. Tim's face barely reached above the frame as he stretched up to look inside to get Charlie's attention. Shaking with the effort of holding himself up, he managed a worried grin. The ground outside was on a steep incline and he balanced carefully on a thin log. Seeing Charlie waving at him he began to frantically wave back. Suddenly, he wobbled and his expression changed to one of sheer terror. His eyes bulged wide open and his mouth fell into a silent cry. All of this appeared to happen in slow motion as he tried his best not to entirely lose control of his balance. However, his footing was lost and he disappeared from Charlie's view. Concerned, Charlie ran to the window and looked down. Tim had fallen face down into a bed of flowers. He remained still for a few seconds then finally lifted his head up and shook the dirt off his face. He turned over and sat up, the sweet smile returning to his face.

'Tim!' Charlie screamed, 'You are an idiot.' With this he skipped to the door and ran outside to meet his dearest friend.

CHAPTER FOURTEEN

THE GWARKS' EXPERIMENT

ROSE SIPPED HER drink delicately and savoured the warm feeling that ran down her throat. She always liked the way the sensation of the ice cold liquid changed to a glowing heat once it slipped beyond her lips. The clear liquid looked innocent but held the strength to turn even the most hardened drinker to a quivering, intoxicated mess. The drink of her choice was not unlike vodka but was extracted from a wild flower that grew in the mountains. Its charm was in the fact that although extremely potent, it never left anyone with a sore head in the morning. The process was slow and intricate, therefore, even a small glass was like gold and was considered to be a drink for celebratory purposes. Harry watched her and marvelled at how this small woman could manage to contain the fiery liquid comet that bolted through her body.

Sitting together in the calm and quiet ambience of the small sitting room, Harry revelled in the fact that he could fully relax in the company of his sister. He did indeed take his responsibilities very seriously but the sacrifice was immense. Long days and sleepless nights were hard going, especially at his age. Even though the Nimarans were physically stronger than humans and lived a lot longer, they too had their limits. Harry was certainly feeling his of late.

Rose regarded her brother, fully aware of how exhausted he was lately. Age was just a minor factor that deteriorated his health; he worked himself to the bone and no matter how much it hurt nothing would stop him…only death.

'So what is going on Harry?' Rose knew that something was bothering him.

Harry remained silent for a moment wondering how much to tell his sister. 'It's the Gwarks.'

'Obviously,' Rose rolled her eyes, 'It is always the Gwarks. What has happened though? I can see by your face, you know something and it is not good news.'

Harry thought back to the early hours of the morning and the sight he witnessed still revolted him so much that he gulped to refrain from throwing up. He knew the Gwarks were violent and cruel but with their own people was too much to accept.

He decided to explain the situation as carefully as possible so as not to upset Rose too much. 'They have started to experiment with our sophisticated devices by themselves.'

Rose looked at him puzzled, 'They have not got the intelligence or aptitude to use anything sophisticated. Surely you cannot seriously believe that this is a threat?'

Harry paused for thought before continuing, 'I do believe it is a threat when they will stop at nothing before they learn how to use them.'

'What exactly do you know Harry?' Rose enquired carefully; the worry tiptoed lightly across her vocal cords causing her voice to quiver uncontrollably.

'You are fully aware that the Gwarks murdered many of our people before learning how to use the various systems and devices that they stole from us. Well, they are determined to learn how to use them. Remember when I told you that Charlie had created a new way of transporting people across distant places?'

Rose merely nodded, anxious to hear more.

Harry tightened his lips together, it was clear that he no longer wished to continue but his captivated audience was waiting. 'Early this morning I was awoken by the alarm going off. Of course, I immediately ran to the source of disturbance which was in one of the central hallways. Some of the others had already got there before me and blocked my view of what all the fuss was about. All I could see was a sea of horrified faces; some clutching their heads in despair, others howling in disgust. Others leant against the walls, doubled over ready to faint or throw up. When my presence was made aware, the crowd parted to reveal something that will always be at the centre of every nightmare that I will have for the rest of my life. A Gwark lay on the floor shivering in pain. He was a complete mess. He had not been transported properly and so his body was completely destroyed. An arm protruded from his mouth and a foot dangled at the side of his head. His skin was non-existent and he bled profusely from every noticeable orifice. His eyes were the worst part of it all, Rose. The terror, panic and absolute pain pierced through those eyes. His death was slow and agonising.

We stopped his misery as quickly as possible but it was not soon enough.'

Harry's words hung in the air like a murky mist that swirled around, poisonous and bitter.

The silence that fell between them was thick. Harry could not rid himself of the picture that was imprinted in his mind;

Rose, shocked and horrified by what she had just been told.

'I am afraid of what their determination will achieve. They have made some progress with the transporter which is a shock. What else can they achieve? We barely beat them before but this time…' Lowering his head, Harry failed to finish the sentence. He could not admit his greatest fears.

'Oh Harry.' Rose groaned and leaned towards him. 'Do not give up hope. What was achieved before will be achieved again. Faith is essential and so is to be even more determined than our enemy.'

Harry smiled at his sister, 'I do not know what I would do without you sometimes.'

'Get some peace and quiet no doubt,' she chuckled needing to lighten the mood that had consumed them.

They attempted to relax once more but it was now strained. Rose gulped the last drops from her glass and decided on a refill. Harry remained intense, staring into space. After a while, he reached out to grab his sister's hand and held on to that comforting touch until the light of day hid below the horizon.

CHAPTER FIFTEEN

NEW FRIENDSHIPS ARE FORMED

THE TWO SUNS shone dazzling white and the three moons created a gentle breeze that made the air warm. The surrounding trees swayed to and fro in a slow waltz as the leaves whispered a delicate rhythm for the dance to follow. Squirrels bounded energetically from branch to branch and at times paused to search inside holes in the bark. Quiet and void of people, nature governed, and each part were at leisure together. The deer moved elegantly over the ground without touching a single flower. Even the bears were light footed, careful of the little insects that jittered around in the soil. All remained ignorant of threat.

Suddenly, a rabbit sat up straight; ears standing to attention as a new noise could be heard in this part of the garden. Very quickly, the rabbit was joined by various other creatures that crowded together in union against the unfamiliar sounds.

Four dots in the distant moved quickly and their sounds became louder.

'And that is how I first met Greg here, the kid who has an aversion to ginger hair, Great.' Bruno finished sarcastically.

All four did not realise that they were being watched by the animals but all too quickly, with curiosity satisfied, the animals fell back into their original wanderings.

Summer, looked around and smiled warmly, 'I like it here. Shall we sit down for a while?' Without waiting for a reply, she placed her jacket on the ground and sat down on it carefully so that it would not get creased. From beneath the jacket, a family of ants ran to safety before her weight settled down onto them. They did not stop running until they had reached the tree line where they felt completely out of danger.

The others joined her.

Greg sat a little distant from the others, in the knowledge that he was not entirely accepted as part of the group.

'So, how old are you Greg?' Elzbieta asked, the sweet tone of her voice was welcoming.

'Twelve,' he replied shyly and bowed his head down. Nervously, he pulled up some of the blades of grass and threw then down carelessly, letting the breeze sweep them some distance away.

'Twelve?' mocked Bruno, 'A bit young to be involved in all this.'

'Sometimes Bruno you act less than twelve years old,' Summer's tone was playful causing Bruno to relax and smile sheepishly.

'Do you know why you are here?' Elzbieta continued, concerned by how little he may know about the circumstances he had been thrown into.

'Harry told me about your previous battle and how you won. He is afraid that another fight might be necessary.' Greg beamed enthusiastically, pleased with himself that he knew more than she did.

Elzbieta had not finished what she was saying and continued, 'And you are entirely happy about being part of this?'

'I was not at first but imagine me, saving the world, for the first time in my life I will be part of something big and important.' His child-like grin matched the innocents of his thoughts.

'You are very brave Greg,' Elzbieta concluded and put out her hand, indicating for him to shake it. 'Welcome to our group.'

His grin widened to the point where his face felt like splitting in two and his eyes shone with joy. Gripping her hand tightly, he shook it with such enthusiasm that caused Elzbieta to bob around due to its force.

'Welcome Greg,' Bruno added and as each member of the group still considered him to be the leader, they followed him in welcoming Greg as a new part of their group.

Greg's grin stretched even further, revealing all of his white teeth. His tongue was sticking out to the side of his mouth and although comical, gave him a rather sweet and childlike expression that made the rest of the group smile. His personality was so pleasant that

Bruno realised he could not help himself to be drawn to the boy.

As Bruno looked at Greg who was now jigging about happily, his eyes caught sight of something behind him. Just a few feet away there was a shimmer in the middle of the space near the tree line, similar to the effect of heat on the horizon. The small circle of space became a blur and appeared to bulge as if something from another dimension was trying to break into it. Bruno began to squint as he tried to make out what it could be. For a few seconds it stopped and then a loud, ear piercing whistle smashed the calm whisper of the leaves; interrupting the motion of the waltzing trees. The space behind Greg began to shimmer once more and the bulge swelled to bursting point. With a loud bang that echoed around the distant hills, a Gwark suddenly appeared. Holding a gigantic laser gun, he snorted and grunted like an angry beast; white smoke bellowed fiercely out of his nostrils. Saliva trickled out of the corner of his wide mouth as he revealed sharp, discoloured teeth. His eyes were lit with the flames of hell and he pointed his hog-like head towards the group. The Gwark broke into a run and charged at great speed towards were Greg was still doing his little jig of excitement. Bruno opened his mouth to warn Greg but nothing came out. He was dumb struck from fear. All he could do was point.

Seeing this, Greg swung around just in time to see the beast who was by then a few feet away from him ready to fire. Instinctively, he spread his arms wide as though he could create a barrier between the Gwark and his new friends to protect them. His face was twisted in terror as he waited for his impending doom. He could feel the nauseous breath across his face and the cold, hard metal that was now pressed against his forehead. He did not even flinch, but became all the more rigid with the determination to save the others. None of them could do anything to help him at that moment but stand and wait for what would happen next.

Then, there was silence.

The Gwark had disappeared.

When Greg realised that he would not die after all and they were all safe, he felt a sense of immense relief. A single tear involuntarily slipped down the contours of his face until it dropped and disappeared into the thick grass by his feet.

The silence continued.

The other three were in a state of shock.

Slowly, Greg turned towards them and in the middle of his forehead was visible a red circle where the gun had been pressed firmly on the soft flesh. Raising a hand and tracing the circle, Greg began to quiver and his lips wobbled uncontrollably. A wet patch formed at his groin and spread down the side of his leg.

The others were all aware of what had just happened but said nothing.

Finally, Bruno announced, 'I think we must go back and see Harry. Greg, you need to go to Charlie's. When you are ready, join us.'

Greg remained in the same spot, pale and silent. Elzbieta walked up to him and carefully planted a soft kiss on his cheek and then, taking him under the arm gently led him back in the direction from which they had just come.

Following behind, Summer took hold of Bruno's hand and quietly whispered, 'did you just see what he did?'

Bruno nodded and quietly replied, 'I can't believe how brave he was.'

'No, it's more than that,' Summer shook her head in disagreement. 'It was not just an act of courage but also out of instinct for the need to protect us.'

Bruno faced her and considered this seriously. 'What a remarkable young boy.'

CHAPTER SIXTEEN

NEW STRATEGIES

'Is this what you really witnessed out in the garden?' Harry raised his voice agitatedly as he spun on his heels and paced the length of his room once more. 'Let me get this absolutely straight, one of the Gwarks materialised from out of nowhere and actually got as far as touching Greg before he disappeared?'

'Well, placed the gun on his forehead.' Bruno corrected him. He had seen Harry in many moods but this unusual outburst of what could only be described as rage, frightened him. No matter what they faced on this planet, Harry always maintained an air of calm and dignity that seemed to suggest that everything would be fine in the end. However, at this moment, he appeared in a panic. If Harry was not to be the voice of reason, who was?

Rose, who was sitting quietly up until now uttered, 'They have improved since this morning.'

Bruno frowned at this statement, 'Are you saying that the Gwarks tried to come here before? Why did you not tell me this?'

Harry sighed deeply and his rage faded away. Bowing his head, Harry then explained, 'One was found in one of the central hallways. I refuse to go into any great detail but an attempt was made by the Gwarks to transport one of them here. They made a big mistake in the process and he did not survive. Now you tell me that they actually transported one of them again but this time successfully in one piece. They are making huge progress very quickly which means that at this rate they could even be here by nightfall. We are not ready to face them and it will be impossible this time to defeat them. There is nothing that we can do.' Wearily, he closed his eyes which suggested that he no longer wanted to speak.

Summer and Elzbieta exchanged a nervous glance. Charlie and Tim, who stood by the window that Tim had tapped on to gain his friend's attention just hours before, could not believe how much could change so quickly. In such a short time what seemed like a distant threat has now become a real one. Fear filled every vein and every artery in their little bodies.

A small voice was suddenly heard from the doorway, 'If I don't want someone to get into my house, I would just change the locks.'

Everyone looked to see who spoke and to their surprise it was Greg. They were all so engrossed in the topic of conversation that they had not seen or heard him come in.

'What are you talking about?' Bruno asked agitatedly.

Greg moved closer to the centre of the room and repeated what he had said but this time a lot more slowly, 'If I don't want someone to get into my house, I would just change the locks.'

All he received was silence.

Huffing, he tried to explain, 'Look, The Gwarks have the key to get into Nimara. That is the transporter that they stole. Now, to stop them from opening the door leading to this place, we just need to change the locks so that their key is useless.'

Charlie's eyes suddenly widened and he skipped excitedly whilst clapping his hands. 'He's got it, Greg has got it! Why did I not think about it? It will be difficult as my invention is very intricate but all of the transporters work on the same principle deliberately so that they can communicate with each other. If they are disconnected, so to speak, then their transporter cannot tap into ours.'

'Are you able to do this?' Harry asked, a slither of hope evident in his voice.

'Yes but it may take time. I will have to start straight away.' Full of enthusiasm and determination he turned to his friend and said, 'Tim, I will need your help. Come on.' With this, the two of them headed out of the room.

'So this may buy us some time but somehow I do not think this will completely prevent the Gwarks from finally unlocking the door, as Greg puts it.' Harry muttered pessimistically.

'My favourite teacher told me that he hated Maths. To stay ahead of the class, he swatted up the night before.' Greg mumbled.

Everyone just looked at him, waiting for an answer to this random sentence.

Realising that the others were waiting for an explanation, Greg attempted once more to make his ideas clearer, 'We know that the Gwarks have got your sophisticated devices and now appear to be equal to you because of this. The only thing they do not have is intelligence and common sense. That is your ammunition. So, use the borrowed time to up your game. Make better weapons that are more superior to the ones that the Gwarks have taken. Stay a step ahead of them at all time.' When he had finished he beamed happily.

Impressed, Harry agreed with Greg's idea and commanded, 'I will summon for the best scientists we have left to attend a meeting in the Great Hall. Bruno, this is your territory again. You will be in charge.'

Bruno felt a strange sensation crawl up his body. Like a furry, black spider, it first stepped onto his toes making him squirm as it touched his nerves. It then slowly explored upwards until it reached his stomach. Here, it built a fluttering web, a network of complicated emotions: panic, fear, self-doubt, and yet excitement, pride and joy. The spider continued its journey and settled on Bruno's mouth where it bit and filled his lips with the venom of silence. He was unable to say anything at all.

★

Harry pressed a button on his desk and spoke quickly. His high pitched squeals still stung the human ears. Within a matter of minutes, Harry was ready to escort them all to the laboratory situated in the Great Hall. Bruno, Summer and Elzbieta were particularly curious to see this room as the name suggested that it should be like the one they had seen in the underground, two years ago. They remembered the room fondly due to how spectacular it was. So many experiments and other activities went on in there. It was decorated with gold pillars and statues. This was Nimara and so they expected the Great Hall to be even more amazing.

Harry led them along corridors that they had not ventured down before and they tried to take everything in, even though the pace felt urgent. Before long they stood before a wall that created a dead end. The wall was golden and appeared to be very dense. It was smooth and unadorned and yet elegant; something very special was behind this wall.

Without saying a word, Harry raised his hands above his head and the wall slid silently upwards, revealing a bright line of light that escaped from the gap on the floor. Already the sound of enthusiastic chatter burst the banks of silence that separated the two rooms. Shadows flickered light fireflies along the increasing gap and Bruno felt his heart drum a staccato beat as he breathed in deeply. The wall had risen to the top and what lay before them was magnificent. This room was as large as the one in the underground but far more structured. Gothic arches rose towards the ceiling which was intricately painted with various scenes that depicted the war that they had fought and won. On close inspection, Bruno, Summer and Elzbieta could see themselves in a variety of portraits. In one, Bruno was immortalised as a brave warrior; fist punched high in the air and his face set in mid scream calling on his soldiers to advance on the enemy. Summer saw herself baring a shield and fighting against a Gwark who was on his knees in defeat. Elzbieta's voice hitched when she saw herself depicted in a white light, looking up to heaven while holding Carlos, who stared up at her lovingly. There was something so angelic, iconic and beautiful that mesmerised her by its sight. The pain of what had happened that moment surged through her, overwhelming her senses that her legs began to buckle from beneath her. Summer caught her before she fell and placed her arm around her shoulders. Elzbieta leaned against Summer to control her whole body from trembling. Carlos, the brave soldier, would always be remembered through this carefully crafted painting.

While everyone was busy engaged in conversation, or actively involved in scientific experiments, Harry moved towards a small group of aliens who stood away from everyone else in the room. It was clear that they did not belong here and Bruno guessed that these scientists were from another part of the planet. He found it strange to consider the fact that there was a whole world beyond this city and he hoped that one day he would be able to visit and explore more of it.

Bruno looked back at Summer and Elzbieta, who were now talking together intimately. He had noticed that just recently they stopped bickering and making sarcastic remarks to each other. He knew that it was mostly Summer's fault and all because of her unfounded jealousy for him. It pleased Bruno greatly that they were now getting on so well. Seeing Summer wipe her friend's tears away with a tissue and whisper soothing words made him love her even more than he thought possible. Her face was softer than it had ever been and the fact that she displayed such tenderness made her all the more radiant and beautiful.

His thoughts were disturbed by Greg tapping him on the shoulder. Turning towards him he found himself face to face with a huge grin. Greg was pointing to various areas of the room with so much excitement that his face had turned bright red. He opened and closed his mouth without getting a single word out. Bruno smiled at this. He understood how Greg was feeling at this precise moment. There was always a continuous surprise, full of delights and wonders waiting to be found in Nimara. Slowly, Bruno let his eyes wonder towards another room across to the one that they were in. The doors were left open and it was in complete contrast to the Gothic features. It was modern, almost futuristic in decor. Chrome and white were the dominant colours and sharp lines replaced curves. Everything was technically brilliant and even the tables were designed for efficiency. Gadgets were removed from draws that swished open and shut smoothly. Water poured from the taps only when they were needed and even the lights seemed to know when to shine brightly or dimly. The place was alive with complicated technology. However, the room still had a sense of charm as the clinical and efficient aspects of it were broken up by creative additions. The floor was a mosaic of tinted glass triangles that fitted together perfectly to form a pattern. It reminded Bruno of a spider's web, woven together by far more talented hands than Arachne herself. The walls were delicately laced with crystals that glinted like little rainbows.

Harry was now walking towards Bruno with the scientists following obediently behind him. Seeing

Harry approach Greg, Summer and Elzbieta instinctively joined Bruno by his side.

'These gentlemen will work diligently in order to meet any requirements that we may have. They are the best that we have now.' Harry clasped his hands in front of him and continued, 'I have told them the situation as it stands with the Gwarks, so they are keen to get on with things as soon as possible. I will introduce you all briefly then I suggest we all rest and meet in the morning. There is much work to be done.'

Harry introduced the first scientist who appeared to be rather shy. He nodded in response but kept his eyes firmly fixed on the floor. A pink hue spread across his cheeks. 'This is Dr Allen, specialising in botanical medicine. He is the founder of cures against 300 different diseases that have plagued many planets in our solar system.' After a brief pause when Dr Allen stepped back, Harry introduced the next scientist. This one was a rather large and grumpy looking alien who muttered to himself from time to time as if constantly arguing with himself. 'This is Dr Stenner, who is responsible for discovering molecule structures for new materials. He has invented metals that are literally indestructible and will be in use for a very long time to come.' Dr Stenner coughed as if clearing his throat and then waddled back to his place in the line. 'Now this is Dr Gaton, a conservationist.' Bruno was surprised by the short introduction but guessed that his job must be extremely important if nothing more was needed to be said. This scientist seemed to be a bundle of energy and leapt forward dramatically before waving frantically. 'Moving on,' Harry continued, 'This is Dr Hallon.'

Bruno was surprised to see that this scientist was a woman. So far the men appeared to be in most of the important positions of power. He found it odd that he had not considered this fact until now. This scientist stepped forward gracefully and smiled sweetly. Bruno wondered what she was known for. He could only imagine it must be something delicate like caring for animals. Harry smiled back and added, 'She is the founding member of a science that is rather new to us and I believe she will be the most helpful to us. Dr Hallon specialises in the invention of new weapons. Her job was created after our last battle.'

Bruno's mouth dropped open in surprise. Again he looked at her and watched as she coyly dipped her head and smiled. Her actions were very feminine in fact almost flirtatious and yet she was responsible for creating weapons of mass destruction.

'And finally,' Harry had moved to the end of the line. 'Dr Broom is devoted to the research of foreign cultures. He enables us to understand and communicate with other races. This is of great importance to us.'

A nervous looking alien stepped forward. He continuously blinked and rubbed the side of his head. 'I am fascinated by your kind.' He started enthusiastically, 'So brutal and incessant liars. It is as though you detest telling the truth. I find this most bizarre.' After saying this he stepped back quickly.

'Thanks, I think.' Bruno responded.

'That's ok.' Dr Broom replied without any intention of sarcasm and then returned to his place with the other prestigious scientists.

'Well, now it is time for all of you to rest. We will meet in my office early tomorrow morning. I will sound the alarm.' Harry then immediately left the room.

Slowly the scientists dispersed.

'I'll walk both of you back to Rose's house.' Bruno told the girls and took hold of Summer's hand.

'I'm coming too.' Said Greg and followed the others as they made their way to the door.

CHAPTER SEVENTEEN

CHANGING THE LOCK

'JUST REMEMBER WE are changing the lock and not removing the furniture inside.' Tim voiced his concern as Charlie tugged on one of the tubes connected to the generator.

'Don't you start with ridiculous metaphors.' Charlie growled through clenched teeth as he strained to reach the button that would release the tube that he was pulling on.

'I do find humans fascinating.' Tim was deep in thought, 'Their languages are very strange. They say things that they do not mean or say one thing but mean something completely different.'

As the tube popped away from the metal latch, green smoke hissed out of it. It hung in the air like a snake surveying possible victims.

'It is their strange inventions that make me laugh.' Charlie added. 'They are so obsessed with making everything so small. Look at mobile phones for example, they spend most of their time trying to find them. The ladies miss calls because they have difficulty in finding the mobile in their handbag. They often do not work properly.' He was now in full flow and Tim hung on to his every word, nodding and agreeing with each statement. 'They do not have a signal when they really need one and instead of perfecting the model, they bring out a new one. How ridiculous is that?'

Tim joined in by adding his own thoughts on the subject. 'I cannot understand predictive texts. Why create a system that decides what the next word should be when it is never the word that the person wants to use? It does everything but actually predict.'

Charlie shook his head bewildered, 'They really should focus on what is important. They need to put more money and energy into finding a cure for many diseases. Make sure that medicine is provided to the unfortunate people on their planet. Here in Nimara, everyone is looked after.'

Turning his attention to the transporter, Charlie lifted a lid on the side of the box and examined the various buttons and blinking lights that appeared to flash rhythmically. Tim stood close by. 'How long will it take you to change the code?'

'I will stay up all night if necessary.' Charlie replied in a matter of fact way. 'The safety of our planet is in my hands right now.'

'I will stay up with you.' Tim placed his hand firmly on his friend's shoulder and smiled at him.

Charlie appreciated having Tim as a friend. He was there for him when his life fell apart after the battle against the Gwarks. A tear slipped down Charlie's face as he thought back to how futile his life seemed after the death of his family. For him those were the most darkest times when the sheer pain of living through them became so unbearable that the only way was to bring it all to an end. His thoughts then returned to Tim who stopped him from going through with it.

On that day Charlie had felt particularly low as it was his daughter's Birthday. He decided to go and place some flowers on her grave and say a little prayer. After he finished he was about to do the same for his wife when his eyes scanned her headstone. He did not read her epitaph that was printed in gold but stared at the empty space beneath it. They had chosen to be buried together, so the empty space would be filled with his one day.

He could not take his eyes away from that empty space and thoughts started to crowd his mind. He could almost visualise what would be inscribed there. A date materialised from out of his mind. That date was his daughter's Birthday. He could take control and end it there and then. He wanted very much to hold his wife and beautiful children again.

With all the thoughts pecking furiously at his brain, Charlie began, as if in a trance, to walk towards the church to reach the high imposing bell tower. He opened the door slowly and walked through a side entrance with winding stairs. Charlie climbed up to the top and felt the rush of wind blow through the windowless arches with the big, heavy bells that swayed slightly. Reaching the edge, he looked down to the bottom where everything seemed very small. He prepared himself to jump when suddenly a voice called out to him, 'I wouldn't do that if I were you.' It was Tim. He knew that Charlie would visit the graves on this special day and decided to join him. He had followed him all the way up to the bell tower.

'And tell me why not?' Charlie asked blankly.

There was a slight pause and then came the answer that stopped him in his tracks. 'You would make one hell of a mess.' Tim replied logically.

Charlie turned to face his friend and seeing the look of concern burst out laughing. He laughed so hard that he thought he would never stop. He laughed all of the frustration and pain and hopelessness until finally, the laugh turned into tears. He slumped down onto the floor and Tim ran to him and put his arms around him and let him cry until he had no more tears left to shed. This was the start of his healing process and Tim remained a blanket of comfort throughout.

With this memory in his mind, Charlie turned to Tim and said, 'You truly are an amazing guy.'

Tim smiled eagerly and rolled his eyes a little shy from getting the compliment.

Together they worked continuously on the transporter, careful not to harm any of the delicate mechanism or wipe out the various codes needed to make the whole machine work. At times they paused to clear their heads or to discuss what the next step should be.

While everyone else was soundly asleep, the two of them worked through the whole night. Tim nudged Charlie when he appeared to be drifting off to sleep and Charlie poked Tim to make sure that he also stayed awake.

The night was peaceful and very still. Only one other light was switched on in the city and that was from Harry's room. The twinkling stars in the dark sky provided no sense of comfort or calm for him. He stood motionless surveying the many houses and skyscrapers that lay across the city, wondering anxiously what life had in store for the people that were living in them. Would Nimara come through this crisis victorious or defeated? Through bloodshot eyes, he watched the movement of the trees as they swayed gently, pushed by the hands of the gentle breeze. He could hear the lullaby of the distant waterfall that called him to his bed. Sleep would have been welcoming as he felt exhausted. However, the burden of responsibility weighed heavily in his heart and his mind was too active to relax. His body, although weak had to keep up with the unfailing energy of his mind.

With patience, as thin as tracing paper, he awaits news from Charlie and considers how much the sweet, young alien has grown as a person. Who would have thought that he would prove to be essential to the fate of the Nimaran race?

Harry had decided that Charlie's future, if they did indeed have a future, would be a very successful one. He would one day lead men and take a high position of power; it was what he was destined for.

CHAPTER EIGHTEEN

BRUNO'S DREAM

BRUNO WAS EXHAUSTED and went to bed early. He knew that the next day would be extremely busy and needed to keep his strength up. So much had happened that he could not take it all in and so as he slept his mind flicked through the events like a recorded film on fast forward. He could see himself tearing at the wrapping paper and then ending up in the empty room. The next moment he was in the chapel looking up at the statue of granddad which then changed to him staring at Charlie's dragon, frozen with fear. The image of Greg boldly standing between the Gwark and the rest of them popped up in his mind which switched to meeting the scientists.

Everything suddenly went blank and darkness filled the screen in his mind.

Slowly a new picture emerged, starting with a bright light that was so intense that in his sleep, Bruno's face winced automatically. It then faded into a brilliant sunlight that reminded him of beautiful summer days.

As the picture became more focused, fields of golden corn surrounded by green hills swayed with the motion of the wind. All of a sudden Bruno was standing in the middle of the cornfield and felt the brittle heads brush against his hands and wrists. The air was warm and smelled fresh and clean. Above him, rolling clouds moved smoothly across the azure sky.

In the distance, he noticed a person standing still, facing the opposite direction so that he could only see the back of him. This person wore a light cream suit and a straw boater that sat snugly on his head, slightly angled to the left. The man appeared to be staring at something in the distance and was totally unaware that he was not alone. Curious, Bruno began to walk towards that man. For no reason at all, he felt drawn to him even though he was anonymous.

As he closed the distance between them, Bruno could make out finer details. He could tell that the man was elderly even though he had good posture and there was something regal about his stance. The way he gently moved his hand up to his head and removed his hat was delicate and yet far from feminine. His hair was pure white and the sun's rays found silver threads that glinted like glitter. Combed neatly, every one of those strands was secured just in the right place and Bruno could swear that he could smell toothpaste and aftershave in the passing breeze. Holding the hat between his fingertips, the man's watch caught the light and reflected its beams so that they winked brightly.

Bruno's breath caught in his throat and he stopped walking forward. His eyes widened and his mouth fell open. Granddad! The single thought boomed loudly inside his mind. Granddad! He broke into a run and even in his sleep, he murmured quietly, 'Granddad'. In his dream this was a loud scream and the man turned around when he heard his name. Smiling broadly, he let the hat fall from his fingers and stretched out his arms, ready to enfold the boy in his arms. Bruno ran so fast that his lungs burned and a stitch was increasing in the side of his rib cage. Still, he kept up the pace and soon collided with the man who wrapped his arms securely around him.

'Dear boy, calm down will you.' Granddad laughed, 'You nearly knocked me over.'

Cuddling tightly, Bruno felt tears well up in his eyes. They stung until they burst and flooded down his face. Grinning with excitement he opened up his senses to capture every scent, every detail of Granddad's face and the feel of his strong, loving arms. He remained like this for some time not wanting to break the precious moment. Granddad patiently just hugged him closely and from time to time let out a small, contented laugh.

Finally, Bruno was ready to talk, 'I went to bed at night hoping that you would come to me in my dreams, but you never came. Why now?'

'I guess you did not need me until now.' Granddad answered soothingly. 'You have got on with your life which I am pleased to see. I am so proud of you and what you have achieved Bruno. You have become a fine young man but then again I knew you would.' Saying this, he patted the boy's head and stood back in order to look at him more clearly. 'I can see that you are no longer a boy, you must be seventeen now.'

Bruno nodded and staring into Granddad's eyes with admiration said, 'I missed you so much.'

'But you coped and carried on.' Granddad smiled and playfully punched Bruno's arm. 'You will also cope with your new situation too. So, the Gwarks are back then?'

Bruno lowered his head and muttered, 'Unfortunately, they are. This time they will be stronger and it will be impossible to win this battle against them.'

Granddad raised his voice slightly, 'Not impossible Bruno, difficult but not impossible. You have courage and clear thinking on your side. You have a bond with your friends which will serve you well. The Nimarans are intelligent and proud people. Together, you are a force to be reckoned with. Defeat is not an option Bruno; you did it before and you can do it again. Have faith in your friends and believe in yourself. Only negative thoughts will prevent you from defeating the Gwarks.' Granddad held Bruno by the shoulders and gazed at him earnestly.

Bruno paused and then in a quiet voice asked, 'Are you in heaven?'

Granddad shook his head, 'You should not have to ask such a question my lad. You should know with your heart that I am.'

'Are you with your wife, Sophie?' Bruno would not be stopped.

Granddad merely nodded and his eyes shone with love at the mention of her name.

'What's it like? In heaven, I mean?' Bruno continued.

Granddad began to walk and replied, 'You know that I am not here to discuss what heaven is like. Many years to come, you can find out for yourself.'

Bruno followed Granddad and side by side they ambled along slowly, slipping through the corn as they went.

'Charlie is working on buying you more time which is needed to be honest. Use that time wisely and prepare yourself as much as you possibly can. Once you are focused you plan good strategies, very creative ones too.' He smiled amusedly as he remembered what training Bruno put the poor Nimaran soldiers through.

'Tell me, what plans do you have this time? Talk me through some of those ideas that are brewing up in your head.' Granddad stopped and sat on a large rock. Bruno decided to join him.

'I don't want to talk about that,' Bruno moaned.

Granddad smiled once more and replied, 'You know that I am here to help you. You want to sort out the ideas that are buzzing around inside of your head, which is why I am in your dream right now. You called upon me not the other way round.'

Bruno sat in silence for a little while and then began to share his ideas with Granddad who listened intently and occasionally asked questions and at other times gave words of encouragement and support. When he finished, Bruno felt a lot better. Exhausted but more confident in himself, Bruno turned to face Granddad one more time. He took in every detail of the gentle man seated next to him. Every wrinkle, every twitch of muscle around his smiling mouth and the sparkle in his eyes that held the signs of wisdom. Bruno felt loved and protected; he felt safer than he ever did before.

After a long silence, Bruno uttered, 'Why do I remember you best in my dreams?'

Granddad's smile faded into seriousness, 'because that is when you have the most time to remember me.' Patting Bruno lightly on his arm, his expression said more than words could ever say. It told Bruno that everything would be alright. That Granddad was extremely proud of him and that he truly loved him like a Grandson.

Bruno just managed to place his arms around Granddad and whisper, 'I love you.'

Waking sharply, Bruno sat up in his bed; he could feel the tears on his cheeks. Looking towards the window, he could see that a new day had began to dawn and sunlight was pushing its way through the curtain. Raising his legs towards his chest, he wrapped his arms around them and placed his head down on his knees, 'I miss you Granddad.'

Then, the alarm sounded.

CHAPTER NINETEEN

PROGRESS IS MADE

BRUNO JOINED HARRY and the five scientists at a long table in the Great hall. They were all deep in conversation and failed to see him standing by one of the chairs. He barely listened but noticed that the table was set with pens, note pads and drinking glasses for every one present. He waited for a moment and then grabbed a pen and tapped it on the empty glass before him. Everyone stopped at once and faced him, except for Dr Stenner, who appeared to be even more in a bad mood than the day before, still muttering to himself.

Harry stood up and welcomed Bruno to sit down, 'I hope that the others will be here in a moment as there is so much to get through today.'

'I am sure that the others will be here in a minute. I asked Greg to fetch Summer and Elzbieta. I wanted to talk to you first.' Confidence oozed from him and his physical presence was felt by all the members of the team around the table. They looked at ease and were captivated by his company and prowess as a leader. Bruno was pleased to see this as he needed their total trust and respect. He knew that he had a huge responsibility to ensure all of them that his plan against the Gwarks would prove victorious. Inside, however, he felt very nervous but had no intention of showing it.

Harry merely smiled at Bruno and whispered, 'I see that you are ready to do your duty. Proceed.' He sat down as a sign that all attention must be focused on Bruno.

Bruno nodded and remained seated, 'You all have great talents and great minds. Each of you is an attribute to me and I am so grateful for that. I have some plans in place to move us forward and I will give each of you specific tasks. However, we are a team and must remain so. At each stage we must communicate with each other, share ideas and not be afraid to speak our minds. If it is clear to one of us that something will not work, speak up. Everyone's thoughts and ideas are precious and necessary.' Bruno paused dramatically and checked that he still held the attention of his audience. He surveyed each of them around the table and could see that all eyes were fixed on him. They waited eagerly for him to continue. He looked at Harry who smiled and nodded approvingly. This gave Bruno the strength to carry on in giving out his final demands. 'Dr Hallon, you are in charge of improving all weapons. Dr Stenner will work closely with you as he can provide new materials to make them better. Each gun, each bomb and everything that we need to fight with against the Gwarks must be improved and be far more superior.'

The two scientists exchanged glances and then nodded in agreement.

Bruno then continued to say, 'Dr Broom, you will deal with any possible communication with the Gwarks. I doubt it if you can bring peace through diplomacy but you may gain some insight into what they are actually capable of and perhaps their strategies. You will need Harry by your side; his experience will be your guide.' Without pausing for a response he added, 'Dr Allen, we will need to prepare medicines and perhaps some miracles. The Gwark army is huge in numbers and many of our men were lost in the last battle due to bad injuries and death. I am counting on you to tend the injured quickly, efficiently and effectively so that they can go back to fight as speedily as possible. Dr. Gaton will work with you. I am sure his knowledge of plants and herbs will be of great help in fulfilling the task.'

'If I may, I'd just like to add something at this point please?' Dr. Gaton stood up and began waving his hands around as he spoke. 'I am concerned about the protection of the environment. I imagine the fight will take place here in Nimara? If so, I do not want to see all of the hard work that we put into rebuilding our cities destroyed again. It just cannot happen. The same applies to our wildlife and vegetation.'

'You are right, precautions must be taken to save Nimara from repeating the horrific damage sustained in the previous war. The subject on this matter leads me to my next plan. I want our men to be sent to the Gwarks planet to fight. We will be a force to reckon with as they will not be expecting us to attack. They think that your race is more interested in avoiding battle at all costs and if this is not possible then to defend itself. To attack would confuse them.' Bruno stopped at this point and waited to see what reaction he would get. At first there was a thoughtful silence and then to Bruno's amazement, one by one, they all agreed. It was clear that they were nervous and uncertain but they had to put their trust in him. He had saved them before and he was determined to do so again. They had to admit that what he said made sense.

'Hey, you started without us.' Greg's voice shattered the atmosphere which had become intense.

Behind him, Summer and Elzbieta came forward holding bulging sacks. Straining they placed each one on to the table.

All eyes were on the sacks.

Elzbieta pointed to the sacks and explained, 'Rose, thought we may need energy. I think we brought enough to feed the whole of Nimara.'

Harry chuckled, 'Good old Rose; so thoughtful. Well, before we carry on I suppose we have to see what she has given us.'

It did not take long for the table to be covered with the various cakes and savoury dishes and soon the notepads and pens were placed on the floor next to the chairs to make room for the fare. It was obvious that Rose's efforts were appreciated but each of the team were eager to get on with the meeting and so the food would be there to pick at rather than enjoyed with the attention it deserved. However, it did create a livelier and less formal atmosphere and everyone's enthusiasm meant that ideas would flow more naturally.

'When do you want to send our soldiers to fight the Gwarks?' Harry asked whilst choosing one of the cupcakes before him. He picked one up and held it in one hand carefully but his eyes remained on Bruno.

Bruno thought about this carefully and replied. 'I imagine that the soldiers have not really kept in that good a shape since the last battle. Their minds were focused on rebuilding the cities and towns and so would not have considered general day to day exercises expected of an army. Am I right to think that?'

Harry nodded slowly, 'Yes that is true. The threat was over and we were at a time of healing.'

'So, we must train them up again. I also imagine we have new recruits as well.' Bruno posed this statement as a question and again Harry nodded. 'In that case, at the very least, three intense weeks.'

'Do you think that we could be ready so quickly?' asked Dr Hallon. Bruno could clearly see that she was concerned about her responsibility to create better weapons in such a short space of time.

'Dr Hallon, we do not really know how much time we have and I do not believe that we have the privilege of taking things slowly. Hopefully, Charlie can buy us some time but I suspect that we will have to be very focused and work as quickly as we possibly can.' Bruno stopped and looked at each of the people around the table. 'I suggest that we get things going today. After this meeting, we will all go off in our individual groups and get down to work.'

Harry stood up at this point and the attention was transferred to him, 'I will make sure that Dr Hallon and Dr Stenner have the lab all to themselves. The rest room with a connecting second lab will be purely for the use of Dr Allen and Dr Gaton. The Library with all its facilities will be used by Dr Broom and myself.' He then turned back to Bruno and asked, 'What do you need Bruno? What are you focusing on?'

Bruno looked towards Summer and Elzbieta who were smiling now as though they knew what their task was going to be and liked the familiarity of it. Their eagerness was infectious and Bruno gave a wide grin, 'Sir, do you have an amphitheatre here?'

Harry beamed and clapped his hands together, 'Excellent! I will summon the soldiers together for this afternoon. Of course we have an amphitheatre.'

Bruno bit his lip as he had one more thing to ask, 'Could we extend that invitation to civilians as well? We need as many people as we can get.'

Without saying a word, Harry lowered his head thoughtfully and then nodded.

Everyone felt content as plans appeared to fall into place so easily. Only Greg looked mystified by the whole conversation and of course Dr Stenner who had silently fallen asleep in his chair with a ring of melted chocolate around his mouth.

Suddenly Charlie and Tim came running into the hall. The golden wall had been left open and so their entrance was a complete surprise. From the far end of the room Charlie shouted excitedly, 'We did it. The locks have been changed. The house is once more secure. The Gwarks no longer hold the key.'

Greg grinned happily as this was something that he understood perfectly well. It was the scientists who looked puzzled. Even Dr Stenner was woken up by the loud noise and began to grumble under his breath.

Harry faced the two little aliens who had by now ran up to the table. They looked so tired and it was evident that they had not slept at all. Their energy was fuelled by success alone. Harry knew all too well that the buzz would not last and that the two of them would have to sleep for the rest of the day. 'I knew that you would do it. Well done Charlie and well done Tim.'

'Do you think that the Gwarks will somehow find the way to unlock the code?' Elzbieta asked nervously.

Charlie's face dropped slightly with uncertainty, 'I cannot begin to imagine exactly what the Gwarks can do. They would have never managed to create such a device but now that they can see how it works...' He ended this sentence with a small shrug.

'Nevertheless, you did what you could and we are grateful.' Harry cut in. 'Both of you had better get some rest now. Your services will not be needed until tomorrow morning.'

Charlie opened his mouth as if to protest but harry held his hand up to stop him in his tracks, 'No! You will do as I command. Sleep and be fresh for the morning or you will be completely useless to us.'

Defeated, both Charlie and Tim swung round and started to walk away.

'I will fill you in on everything later,' Harry promised.

Hearing these words Charlie turned back and gave an almighty smile and then swiftly made his exit. Tim followed obediently.

'Do we need to discuss anything further?' Harry questioned, bringing back the attention of the group again.

'I have just one more thing to say,' Bruno replied, 'Please, remember to keep us updated on anything, no matter how insignificant it may seem.'

Everyone agreed to this and began to move away from the table in their small groups.

'Don't forget to take some food with you,' Harry said with a hint of humour, 'There is so much here.'

After the scientists left the room, Harry moved towards the four humans who remained in the room. 'I will personally show you the way to the amphitheatre. I must admit, it feels so good to know that you are in charge of what suits you best.'

Taking the lead, Harry began to glide out of the room and the others followed.

CHAPTER TWENTY

THE NEW AMPHITHEATRE

BRUNO WAS THE first to step into the amphitheatre. He stood just inside the doorway and took in the new surroundings. The lay-out was the same as the one they had in the underground. Rows of seats gradually sloped down towards the stage in the centre of the circle. It was obvious that the stage was the focal point. White stairs were placed from every side so that people could enter from various points around the room. Highly polished wooden panels covered the entire length of the walls. The light bounced off them giving a mirror like effect. The ceiling was very high and thousands of little lamps were drilled into it, giving the whole room an even coating of light. It was clear and bright and yet without causing any discomfort to the eyes. There was no one in the room at that moment except Bruno.

Then entered Summer, who edged her way in by pushing Bruno further into the room making space for Elzbieta and Greg. As Summer looked around with excitement it brought back memories of when she had first entered the amphitheatre in the underground and all the emotions came flooding back. Her reunion with Bruno who she thought was lost to her forever. She remembered the way he looked at her and how they linked hands. It was at that moment when time had stopped and nothing else existed but the two of them. She glanced over at Bruno and saw that he too was deep in thought, a secret smile playing on his lips. Sensing that she was looking at him, he turned towards her and winked cheekily. He was thinking the same thing as she was and this filled Summer with a warm glow.

Elzbieta went straight to the stage and was instantly reminded of the fight she had with Charlie. Angry with the way he was showing off, she had punched him. Guiltily, she remembered how hard the blow was and the poor creature was in considerable pain. She frowned to herself and realised that she had once been a spontaneous girl who acted on impulse, sometimes with violence. Reflecting on her past she realised how much she has changed and become a mellower person.

Greg, however, was seeing everything with new and innocent eyes and was in awe of his surroundings. He spun around in an attempt to see everything at once and pointed here and there while saying ooh and ah every so often. The other three watched him and fully understood what he was feeling at that precise moment. They had reacted in a less melodramatic way when they first entered the room like this but the sentiment was the same.

Together they decided to sit down by the stage and wait for the soldiers to arrive.

Bruno looked at all the seats and calculated that they could possibly fit around five hundred people comfortably. Hopefully that was not the whole army. He was counting on there being at least a thousand. Perhaps Harry chose a select few to start off with.

They did not have to wait long as from behind the door that they had entered, an eruption of noise could be heard as aliens spoke quickly to each other. The door opened and a sea of people flooded in, cascading down the stairs and settling down in the rows of seats.

When everyone was settled, Bruno took centre stage while the other three remained a little further away from his left side. It was his responsibility to address the audience and once again he proved himself to be a confident and trustworthy leader. Scanning the aliens seated before him, Bruno was pleased to recognise many of them. It seemed as though Harry had sent only the soldiers to this initial meeting. This sense of familiarity was comforting and he took in a deep breath before commencing.

'Soldiers, we must remember that not so long ago you all were courageous, willing to fight for your land, your people, your families and the future. You were victorious.' Bruno paused and taking in another deep breath continued. 'It is time to call on your faithful services again. The Gwarks mean to start a war once more. This time, they have your weapons and are stronger for it. This time, you will have to be stronger and braver and more determined to protect your loved ones and the future of Nimara.'

There was an outburst of muttering amongst the crowd so Bruno raised his voice. This proved effective as everyone stopped and focused again on what he had to say.

'I do not believe that you want to see what you have so successfully rebuilt destroyed again. I also do not believe that you want your beautiful environment ruined by warfare. For this reason and many other reasons, I believe action must be taken from our side. We will not wait for them: we will go to them. We will fight on their land and destroy their buildings and ruin their environment instead.'

Total silence met these words. Bruno felt the blood pump through his veins, beating a fast rhythm against his temples. A bead of sweat framed his forehead and his breath quickened. Still, he said no more and waited for some kind of reaction.

Someone at the back of the room started to clap and stood up. Bruno was thankful. Then another person on the back row also started to clap and then stood up. This rippled through the audience until everyone was standing and clapping.

Bruno looked around at each individual in the crowd and smiled with relief; they were on his side.

'As of today you are back in training. Tell your friends and family that I invite everyone who is willing to be part of this. All they need to do is have the courage and the need to defend their own.' Bruno motioned for the other three to join him by his side and obediently they came forward.

'Today, you will be placed into four groups and you will train under the supervision of one of us. You will have time to get to know everyone in your group. Your group will become your family and you will know each other's strengths and weaknesses. Together you will be strong; you will be invincible.'

'A bit over the top. Invincible?' Summer whispered and gave a cheeky grin.

'It's called motivating them.' Bruno whispered back.

Summer raised her eyebrows at Bruno but her humour was still evident.

'How are we going to place them into groups?' Elzbieta asked, leaning over Summer to get Bruno's attention.

'Just randomly,' Bruno replied, 'I have not exactly been given the time to work everything out.'

Then talking to all three of them, Bruno instructed, 'Take a corner of the room each and I will tell each of them which group to go into. They should be equal in size. Once you have your group, take it to another area. I think outside in the garden would be appropriate. Encourage them to talk together, relax and enjoy each other's company. I am serious when I say they need to work together. Tomorrow, we start training, so tonight, we four will devise a timetable. We have three weeks at the most so the plan must be very structured.'

'I get to lead a group?' Greg asked in disbelief.

'Don't worry Greg, you will be fine.' Elzbieta spoke soothingly.

'Oh don't worry about me; I know I will be fine. It's just so exciting that's all.' Greg beamed at the prospect of being in charge.

'You take everything in your stride don't you Greg.' Elzbieta chuckled and gave him a playful punch on the arm.

'Ok, take your corner guys.' Bruno prompted.

It did not take long to place everyone into four groups as the aliens were eager and responsive. Bruno watched as they were all led outside into the sunshine.

He was pleased with how everything had gone so far but felt dread creep up his spine like a venomous snake. This was similar to the way the last practise for battle started and although they won, many precious lives were lost and many hearts broken.

CHAPTER TWENTY ONE

THE SCIENTISTS GET TO WORK

WHILST BRUNO AND his friends were busy sorting out the soldiers, the scientists got settled into their designated areas to get down to work. Dr Hallon led the way eagerly before Dr Stenner who ambled along behind, grumbled quietly to himself. She ignored him and swiftly stepped towards a white sliding door that led to the main laboratory. She moved her hand over the door and it slid open.

The bright white light cascaded out of the room and she winced when it hit her face. Dr Stenner plodded up to her and his hot breath tickled her neck; he wheezed as though he had just completed a marathon.

Stepping inside, Dr Hallon took in everything that was there for her use. She marched towards the table and began to open draws and cupboards, looking through them for items that would be of use to her. Her movements were quick and rhythmic as she pranced joyfully around the room. Touching buttons and turning knobs on various pieces of equipment. She was clearly ecstatic with the room and its arrangement. She took off her lab coat and swung it over a nearby stool and began to place various instruments on the sparkling white table before her. Her movements were as graceful and spritely as Julie Andrews in Mary Poppins. It would not have been out of place for birds and other cute animals to have swooped in for a jolly sing song.

Dr Stenner watched her silently and feeling exhausted by her energy slumped down heavily onto a stool. His large body flopped over the sides of it like congealed lumpy custard whilst his stumpy legs failed to reach the floor. He wobbled from side to side grimacing and heaved his heavy legs up until his heels hooked onto the bar between the stool legs. He snorted, and then opened a bag which contained a large chocolate muffin and began to chomp on it. His face relaxed into an expression of sheer delight as crumbs dropped down the front of his lab coat.

Dr Hallon turned towards Dr Stenner and said, 'Well, it seems we have everything and more than we need here. I think it best we start focusing on improving the most important weapons first and work our way down towards the least essential ones.'

Dr Stenner remained quiet until he finished chewing and swallowing the last bit of the muffin. He brushed the remaining crumbs off his coat and spotting a chocolate chip biscuit, raised his eyebrows and gingerly picked it up between his chubby thumb and forefinger. He looked at it greedily before pushing it into his mouth. 'Guns.' He growled. 'Guns are the most important weapons to begin with. Our soldiers must be equipped with the most superior ones.'

Dr Hallon frowned and waited for her partner to expand on his idea.

Dr Stenner, after a long pause continued, 'The Gwarks are close range fighters. They advance into battle quickly and enjoy close contact with their enemy. They take pleasure in the smell of blood, torn flesh and most of all fear. Guns will allow our soldiers to keep them at a safe distance as well as useful on close contact. We need to create guns that fire accurately and easily at close range of a few inches or distant of about 10 feet or more.'

Dr Hallon pondered over this for a few moments and replied, 'Good idea Stenner but any gun would be clumsy to operate at such close range. How could any of our men load, aim and fire a gun accurately within two inches of the enemy? It's impossible!'

Dr Stenner smirked, 'We are improving the weapons remember. The old fashioned style of gun is of no use to us anymore. Think girl, what is the quickest reflex that anyone has?' With this he took a clamp from the side of the table and threw it at Dr Hallon. Without thinking, she held her hand out flat in front of her and the clamp bounced off from her palm and fell onto the floor between the two of them.

'Are you suggesting we make guns that fit in the palm of the hand?' she questioned.

Dr Stenner's smirk became very smug and he nodded, 'not only to fit in the palm of the hand but be part of the hand, controlled by the mind. The perfect reflex.'

Dr Hallon pulled a stool over and sat next to the large genius, 'So, we need a material which is strong and able to withstand extreme heat. The gun will have to fire laser beams and yet not damage the skin it is embedded in. Also, we have to consider psychological treatment for the soldiers who are going to be fitted with them. They must possess great control when and where they fire the weapon otherwise the outcome could be catastrophic. Is this possible? I mean, can we do this in the short time we have.'

Dr Stenner leaned in and whispered, 'We can do this and so much more. We are the best remember.'

★

Dr Allen and Dr Gaton had just entered the rest room which was close from where Dr Stenner and Dr Hallon were feverously concocting ideas on how to improve various weapons. It was a small and cosy room, decorated in a light shade of pink. The floor was covered in a thick pile carpet that although white, seemed to capture the shade of the pink walls and absorb it into each smooth, silky soft fibre. A large sofa, covered in large pillows took centre stage. Just by looking at the sofa it became obvious that once seated in it, a victim would find it almost impossible to break away from its loving embrace.

This room was void of any technology or electrical gadgets. It was purely for the use of relaxation and reflection. Any disruptions were not allowed here.

Both scientists physically relaxed as they looked around the room. Their shoulders fell back into a more comfortable position and they no longer looked tense. They breathed deeply, allowing the soothing scent of lemongrass to invade their nostrils. They both knew that this room was perfect for the many topics of conversation that they will be having together.

However, even though the rest room held a spell over them, it was not strong enough to quell Dr Gaton's curiosity of the connecting room at that moment; The Lab. He could not suppress his desire to see it any longer and got up suddenly and raced towards the door, whipping it open and stepping inside. He completely disregarded his new partner, Dr Allen, who slowly and bewilderingly followed behind.

The lab was not at all what they had expected. It was not clinical, bright white or filled with straight tables and cupboards. To both the scientists' delight it was like a tropical rainforest, as if by magic they had stepped into yet another world filled with botanical surprises. The damp heat mixed with vegetation gave off a musky scent that was heavy yet not unpleasant. The sound of running water was predominant and yet soothing. Here and there a leaf fluttered or a bush rustled signifying the fact that this room was very much alive. In the corner of his eye, Dr Allen could just capture the quick movement of a shy bird that hid even further into the depths of a nearby tree. With a keen eye, the snout of a small furry creature could be seen poking out of the rustling bush, twitching nervously before retreating back into the shadows created by the dark green leaves that protected it.

The various species of foliage made Dr Gaton's heart race with excitement as this was the love of his life. His whole heart, mind and soul was the environment and he was in a sense married to his job. He turned to his partner, who did not know where to look first as every wonder left him tingling with joy. His eyes were wide and his mouth gaped in a perfect oval.

Frowning, Dr Gaton warned his partner, 'You do not touch anything unless I tell you to. I am not letting you hurt any living thing in this room. Do you understand me?'

Dr Allen switched his attention to the fierce looking alien that stood opposite him and automatically bowed his head down as his eyes studied the floor. Stuttering, he whimpered, 'But part of my job is using life to save life. I need the magical healing powers of these plants in order to cure our kind.'

Dr Gaton glared and replied, 'These innocent plants and trees give so much to the world already, why bleed them dry of everything they have just to serve us. All you want to do is hack them down and rip them to shreds, they have feelings too you know. Their agony may be silent but I hear them, I feel them.'

Dr Allen took a quick step backwards as Dr Gaton moved forward with a tight fist punching the air. The wind created by this movement brushed against Dr Allen. However, even though Dr Allen was feeling nervous and uncomfortable with this situation, he was just as passionate about his purpose in life and courageously argued his point. 'I understand your feelings but it is not only the mistake of the individual that can be detrimental to their health. Sometimes fate deals a nasty blow. Think about the actions of others, how that can influence what harm is placed on an innocent person. Think about diseases that we still have not found the cure for. The complexities of life often leave a person wondering why bad things happen to them or a loved one.'

At the mention of a loved one, Dr Allen noticed his partner flinch. He had touched a raw nerve and so he decided to pluck at it as much as possible in order to settle the argument.

'I imagine someone close to you died recently, most probably in the war against the Gwarks?' Dr Allen posed this statement as a question in order to find that nerve once more. Seeing that this did not get the reaction he had hoped for, he continued to dig.

'Perhaps someone you loved spent days or months in agonising pain as a disease slowly ate away at them physically and mentally?'

A tear welled up in Dr Gaton's eye and tumbled down the side of his face. He turned pale but tried hard to conceal his emotion. It was futile as his inner pain was stronger, causing his small body to shake.

Dr Allen realising the cause of Dr Gaton's anguish continued relentlessly, 'Your mother.' Those words were all that he needed to get the reaction he was waiting for.

'My Mother was an angel. She lived a healthy, good life. She ate well and loved walking. It was age that took her. Her body grew tired and so did her mind. Her bones began to weaken to the point that one touch could break them and she bruised so easily. Then, she started to forget things. We just shrugged it off thinking that it was due to her age. Then, we thought it was funny when she put the phone in the fridge or put her slippers in the oven. Then...' Dr Gaton gave a weary sigh as he found the next words almost impossible to say out loud, 'Then... she forgot who I was and in fact she became frightened of me. I was a complete stranger.'

Dr Gaton stared at his partner who listened patiently. 'None of the scientists could do anything. They were all useless, absolutely useless. We are such an intelligent race, superior to any other living planet and yet I had to watch my mother suffer for months, frightened and in pain and I could do nothing.'

Carefully, Dr Allen pushed the sensitive conversation in the direction he wanted, 'We have a chance now to stop others from suffering like your mother did. I know that we will never be able to beat death and I know that in time new diseases will baffle us in the future but we must do the best that we can now. We have the chance to make amazing advancements with all this around us.' He pointed at the magnificent garden around him. 'We have determination and we have each other's talents. We must work together. I promise to be very careful with the plants and other gifts in this room. Anything that you do not want me to do, I will listen and respect your wishes. Please, all I ask is that you respect mine too.'

Dr Gaton paused for a moment as if considering what his partner had said and reluctantly, still not totally convinced held out his hand. Dr Allen shook it, smiled gently and then asked, 'What happened to your mother in the end?'

Dr Gaton replied slowly, 'I pretended that I was her nurse and behaved accordingly. I never mentioned that I was her son ever again and that seemed to work. When she took her final breath, I was beside her and when I was absolutely sure she could not hear me, I told her that I loved her more than anything in the whole world and that I was grateful for each day I had with her.' Dr Gaton's smile was full of sorrow.

Dr Allen's heart broke for him and therefore, decided that he would never broach on the subject again.

All focus was on what they could achieve in the three weeks that they had left before the battle commenced against the Gwarks. All their energy would be placed on their efforts into healing wounds quickly and with minimal pain and introducing new ways of successfully keeping their patients alive. Of course they knew nothing about the ideas that were taking shape in the weapons department just three corridors down. They were too busy concentrating on their own particular niche of knowledge.

Dr Allen became thoughtful and said, 'We need something that will cauterize wounds immediately if we are to keep our soldiers on the battlefield.'

Dr Gaton quickly began to protest against the idea by saying, 'Cauterize wounds, is that all? After everything we just spoke about you can only think about basic projects. I was thinking more in the line of fixing legs and arms that have been chopped right off. I am talking about healing gaping chest wounds from the laser guns that melt away solid flesh and bone. I am talking about bringing our soldiers back from the brink of death.'

Dr Allen looked at the enthusiastic scientist before him and licked his lips thoughtfully. 'Yes, I know that somehow we will have to find ways of making miracles and find effective medical procedures to achieve all these things but first we will have to make sure that our soldiers lose as little blood as possible and the rest will hopefully follow. Divine intervention would also help, after all it will be in Gods hands if a soldier lives or dies.'

Dr Gaton blinked and stood stunned by what he was hearing, 'I am aware of that.' He protested with a firm voice, 'But God gave us the ability and the materials to make those miracles work. His gifts of medicine and our knowledge of perfecting it are our best tools. Nature is our friend and if we treat it kindly and respectfully, it will be our guide, inspiration and salvation.'

★

On the other side of the huge building, close to the Central Hall, Harry and Dr Broom were seated in the library. They had already settled into a deep conversation before any of the other scientists had even begun to find the rooms that they would be working from. They sat in magnificent, high backed leather chairs. The deep green seats were surrounded by a wooden frame work that was carved into shape with such precision that from any angle it could only be admired as a thing of beauty. Between them was a low table of the same wood and appeared to have been carved by the same hands as the chairs.

The walls surrounding them were completely filled from floor to ceiling with books. They were arranged alphabetically but also in thematic order. There were old, thick leather bound books next to modern thinner texts and the colours created a chaotic pattern across the room. The smell of old paper was enticing and dared anyone to select a book and spend a fulfilling time reading. The floor was made of deep red tinted oak.

There were small computers discreetly tucked away in various areas of the room. Although they looked insignificant compared to the bold statement given off by the books, they held vast amounts of information. Any question could easily be answered by the touch of the button as years upon years of research and study were stored in the multitude of files inside the intricate software.

'So, you want to communicate with the Gwarks? What do you hope to achieve through this?' Dr Broom was always pessimistic about the nature of man and although every species intrigued him, he did not believe that anyone apart from Nimarans held any good qualities in which to appeal to. This was often viewed as a contradiction in terms to his profession yet his negativity created a yearning to be proven wrong. He studied cultures with the eagerness and the will of a dying man who wanted proof of an afterlife. He grasped at tiny fissures of hope that may lead to buried, deep rooted emotions of empathy, compassion and forgiveness. So far, in the Gwarks, he found only one. This was the reason why he was so fascinated by the humans that inhabited Earth because in his study so far, he found a glimmer of hope, especially after hearing the passionate way that Harry spoke about the visitors and what they had achieved in the last battle. He still held reservations and mistrust for them but nevertheless it led to his curiosity to challenge himself and his studies.

Harry responded to Dr Broom's question in a manner that showed the answer was clearly obvious, 'I hope that we can prevent war again. Diplomacy could very well be the answer. If we show willingness to forgive and reach some kind of understanding and tolerance between us and the Gwarks, then perhaps we can live harmoniously, in spite of our differences. Of course, I do not suggest that we could ever be friends but at least leave each other alone.' Harry picked up his glass from the table before him, swivelled the ice cubes around the amber liquid and then took a large gulp of the drink. He gasped with satisfaction as the liquid warmed the path it travelled along down his throat.

After listening attentively, Dr Broom replied, 'In my studies I have found that they are a strange community. They only care about their immediate families but have zero tolerance towards anyone outside their own circle. Not a nice race of people.' Dr Broom looked at his drink that sat on the table within arms reach but did not pick it up as he continued. 'At least there is the slight chance that there may be something to work on. They do have a redeeming aspect in their nature when it comes to their total loyalty towards their own families. The Earth people on the other hand do not always have these sentiments towards their own.'

Harry shook his head slowly, 'Dr Broom, please can we just focus on the Gwarks. As I said before, you are much too harsh on the humans.'

Unconvinced, the scientist muttered under his breath but kept to the conversation on the Gwarks. 'They lost many in the battle and perhaps this is something we can appeal to. Would they really want to lose more? I also believe that now they are starting to realise that we can be fighters too. Their pride was hurt last time surely they would be more cautious this time?'

Harry questionably replied, 'It is this caution that worries me. I also do not understand how they managed so quickly to work out the technical designs of our weapons and even more so the transporter. I am even nervous that they will break the new code set by Charlie. There is more to this than meets the eye, but I just cannot see what. How could they have advanced suddenly to such an extent intellectually? It just does not make sense.'

'Yes it does seem very strange when you put it that way and it is unnerving indeed.' Dr Broom commented, which did not give Harry any sense of confidence at all. 'I will look at the background history and see what other battles they may have lost in the past and I will also try to find out who they have formed alliances with and for what reasons. I will dig up as much information as I can find and then we will contact the Gwarks. As a matter of interest, have you considered who we should appeal to?'

Harry placed the glass back down on the table and looked seriously at Dr Broom, 'Go to the top. The woman in charge.'

CHAPTER TWENTY TWO

THE TRAINING TIMETABLE

IT HAD BEEN a very busy day for Bruno but he was pleased with its outcome. His team of soldiers appeared to accept whatever was required of them and with enthusiasm they had spent the time in the garden effectively. They all got to know one another, shared stories, mutually laughed and even sympathised and cried together. They were bonding as a team. Bruno was pleased to see that some of them had begun to share their talents with each other and interestingly enough friendship groups started to form. The mass of people became divided into sections. Some grouped together according to the similarity in their abilities, others through the love of deep conversation. One of the groups disappointingly appeared to be idle and sat staring up at the sky or fumbled with their hair, hands or attire and hardly spoke to anyone. Bruno would have to find a way of motivating them. He needed each and every one of them to make the stand against the Gwarks a success. It all seemed as though once they found others of a similar disposition as their own, that was where they felt the most comfortable.

By watching them, Bruno found it easier to decide where their place in a battle would be. He had already decided that he would use the same strategies as last time. All he had to do was build upon them and make them better.

It was nearing evening now and sitting on his bed in Charlie's apartment, his thoughts turned to the other groups and wondered how they were getting on. He was absolutely sure that Elzbieta would be regarding her team with as much vigilance as he was. He could just picture her mingling amongst them, asking questions and making sure that they all mingled with each other. She would be making notes on a pad of paper in order to provide him with much needed information. This made him smile to himself and chuckle.

Summer would be enthusiastic and take her responsibility seriously but her methods would be scattier. It never ceased to amaze him that her chaotic disorder, although frustrating to him, always seemed to work. He could not imagine what she was getting up to with her group. All he could envisage was her sweet smile, her long flowing hair that caught the rays of the sun. He imagined her energetically skipping around and laughing with the aliens as they looked up at her with adoration. His smile had softened with these thoughts. He loved Summer so much and knew that one day she would be his wife. As Granddad had said, 'Love grows.' Granddad sure knew what he was talking about.

Bruno turned his attention to Greg. He was still new to the group and Bruno felt very unsure of how the day went for him. The aliens seemed eager to accept his place in command and he had shown strength and confidence but time would tell. The one thing Bruno was sure of and that was he respected Greg for his intelligence and loyalty. Without question he had thrown himself into every challenge set before him; he was truly remarkable.

There was a light tap at the door and Bruno instinctively looked up. Slowly, the door opened and a tired looking Charlie poked his head in and smiled drowsily at Bruno.

'You slept well.' Bruno remarked, 'Come in and sit down.'

Charlie took two steps into the room and then yawned. His mouth gaped open and his arms stretched above his head. Once this was finished he rubbed his eyes with clenched fists and grinned at Bruno. His movements were as innocent as a baby. With a little more vitality, Charlie moved towards the chair opposite Bruno and sat down.

'So, what did I miss?' Charlie asked. It was clear that he was frustrated by the fact that he had not been involved with anything that had happened that day.

'I thought Harry was going to fill you in' Bruno teased his friend, 'Don't you want to go and see him?'

'You know I can't wait and anyway, Harry will be too busy at the moment. He is always too busy.' Charlie quipped. He stared at Bruno and folded his arms. His little legs dangled inches above the floor and swayed back and forth.

After this Bruno stopped taunting Charlie and replied, 'Honestly, you did not miss that much. The scientists you saw around the table this morning are all working on creating better weapons and developing medicines. I think Harry is thinking about contacting the Gwarks in order to try and settle things without going into battle.'

'That sounds like what Harry would want to do.' Charlie agreed, he paused for a moment and then asked, 'What have you organised Bruno? What is your plan?'

Bruno looked at his little friend who was clearly waiting for a reply, 'Summer, Elzbieta, Greg and I have started to put an army together. Tonight we will be going over a training timetable.' He stopped abruptly and did not know how to tell Charlie about his more ambitious idea. He could see Charlie sitting up straight in the chair and searching for clues in his face eagerly. He knew there was something more to be said and waited impatiently.

Bruno continued cautiously, 'This time, the army will go to the Gwarks. We want to have the element of surprise on our side.'

Charlie's eyes widened, partly due to the prospect of invading the Gwarks planet but also with the thrill and excitement of being part of something so dangerous and daring. Bruno could read him easily and the expression on Charlie's face was what he feared. He wanted to protect Charlie this time around as he had been through too much already.

'Of course, I will be coming with you...' Charlie began.

'No! Not this time.' Bruno raised his voice causing Charlie to stop in mid flow and blink in astonishment. Calming down, Bruno explained, 'You are the only person I trust and rely on to keep control of the transporter. You built it and therefore you will be the one to beam us up.'

'I keep telling you, it does not work in that way, it is a sophisticated...' Charlie was visibly annoyed by this.

'Whatever, I would rather not know how it works actually.' Bruno cut in once more. 'I want only you at the controls, no-one else.'

Charlie fell into a stunned silence and finally muttered, 'Tim could do it.'

Bruno raised his eyebrow at Charlie denoting the end of the conversation, however, Charlie chose to ignore this and spoke most earnestly, 'I have always stood by you.'

To Bruno's relief there was a loud knock on his door and in a cheerful voice Greg shouted, 'Can we all come in?' Before Bruno could reply the door opened and Greg barged his way in with a beaming smile. Summer and Elzbieta followed behind him.

Greg went straight to Bruno and sat on the bed beside him, 'I went to pick these two up and Rose asked me to try one of her new cakes. She has decided to experiment with vegetables now. She says if you can have carrot cake then you can use anything in a cake. I had beetroot cake but to be honest it was a bit weird.'

'All that woman ever seems to do is bake.' Summer added.

Summer and Elzbieta remained standing by the door as the room was not large enough to accommodate more chairs. Seeing this Bruno swiftly stood up and asked, 'Shall we go to the lounge? There is more space there.'

Charlie switched his attention from Greg to Bruno and nodded frantically in agreement, 'Of course, good idea. Just go straight in and I'll bring in some snacks.' Before he had even finished the sentence, Charlie had jumped up and walked out of the door with a sudden vitality that surprised Bruno. Just moments earlier he was barely keeping his eyes open.

They all left the room and Bruno led them into the lounge. Summer and Elzbieta gasped as they took their first steps into the room.

'It is beautiful.' Elzbieta whispered as her eyes swept over the whole room, stopping for only a few seconds to give more attention to individual details that stood out to her.

Summer went straight over to the sofa and sat down. She ran her hands over the arm rest, adoring the velvet texture and mouthed, 'Wow.' She picked up one of the plump cushions and held it tightly like a teddy bear and settled comfortably into position. She noticed the black sheet on the wall and frowned as if trying to work out why it was hanging on the wall.

'It is a television.' Bruno told her. 'It has an amazing picture. I have never seen anything so clear in all my life. I would show you but Charlie clicks his fingers and it comes on. I don't think it would work for me.'

On hearing this Greg clicked his fingers and immediately an image came to life on the sheet. A male and female alien were caressing in a loving embrace and talking quickly. Of course, Bruno did not understand the language but it was obvious that it was a romantic film. For some reason it humoured Bruno to think of aliens getting emotionally drawn into something like this. Again, the sound and picture were crystal clear and the two girls watched the screen in awe.

Greg clicked his fingers again and the screen turned instantly blank.

Charlie entered the room with a tray filled with bags of crisps and sweets. On the edge of it were perfectly balanced glasses full of lemonade. The bubbles popped and sprayed like fireworks above each glass and the cubes of ice created a dance to the rhythm of Charlie's movements as he carefully scuttled over to the table to put the tray down. A pile of sandwiches formed a tower in the middle.

Once this was accomplished and everyone had settled down around the table, Bruno began to speak, 'From tomorrow and the rest of the week, I want us to focus on each soldier's abilities and make sure they are finely tuned to the utmost limit of perfection. We all know that they are all immensely fit, so we do not need to waste time on that. This, in turn, will help us to start forming strategies for when we actually go into battle.'

Greg who was sitting on the floor had to stretch his hands up towards the table in order to pluck a sandwich from the tray while at the same time keeping his attention firmly focused on Bruno.

'So, we need to fine tune the abilities of the soldiers we already know and find out what the new guys are capable of doing and make sure that they are of the same standard.' Elzbieta confirmed.

'Exactly,' Bruno replied enthusiastically. 'I don't think we need to get the new men used to how bloody the battle can get like we did last time. Most, if not all of them witnessed the violence two years ago and I doubt that the experience would be forgotten too easily. In fact, I am very shocked that they all seem prepared to go into battle at all. Last time they did not have a clue what they were going to face, not really but this time…' Bruno stopped mid-sentence, unable to express his train of thoughts.

'We are all frightened but the desperate need to protect our land, our people keeps us going Bruno. We are Nimarans and if we do not make a stand, we will all die and our entire world. We do not have a choice.' Charlie answered sorrowfully but his determination and strength was evident.

For a few moments everyone was silent and only the quiet noise of crunching could be heard as Greg bit down on the crunchy salad in his sandwich.

Bruno decided to resume with the first topic, 'During the week, I will see what the scientists have come up with and this will dictate the next step of training we will take. I imagine we will have to get used to new weapons, and when they are ready that will become top priority.' Grasping his glass, he paused to take a large gulp of the tangy drink. The others waited in silence. 'Is everyone clear on what they have to do tomorrow? Greg, I will fill you in on the kind of things we did last time.'

The rest of the group were happy with the plan so far and began to relax.

Herbert the dragon, who was in his room nearby, woke up upon hearing the sounds of laughter and quickly lifted his head and pricked his ears up. He had been chained to the wall of his cave to prevent him from disturbing the meeting and the chain rattled with his movement. He realised that he could not leave his room to investigate and gave a disappointed whimper. Despondently, he lowered his head once more and sighed heavily.

From the far corner of the room, a shadow suddenly moved and looked like it was dancing to the rhythm of a flickering light. The dragon watched this sleepily but his eyes opened wide when the shadow began to take form. Within seconds the Gwark materialised fully and began to run towards the dragon. He had an axe which he held high above his head and his hog-like face was contoured with rage. He managed to get within a few feet of Herbert before the dragon lifted his head, breathed in deeply and then exhaled fire at the Gwark who instantly became a pile of ashes. Absently, the dragon swung his tail towards the pile of ash and brushed it until it almost disappeared completely.

CHAPTER TWENTY THREE

CONTACT IS MADE

IT WAS NOW morning and it had become the norm for Harry to sleep no more than a few hours. He paced around his office impatiently. For a few moments he stopped at his desk and looked at the computer screen and then continued with his agitated walk from one side of the room to the other. After doing this several times, he shook his head and then pressed a button on the screen which caused a huge black, stiff sheet to descend from the ceiling. When the sheet got to the middle of the wall it stopped. It was very similar to Charlie's television screen but more impressive.

Placing his hands behind his back in an attempt to stop them from shaking, he began to pace the room once more. Harry's heart banged furiously in his chest, the violence of it caused his tiny frame to jolt with every thump. He was not at all looking forward to talking with his enemy. However, if there was any chance of resolving the situation peacefully, it had to be done.

Dr Broom entered the room without knocking and gave a nervous grimace.

Harry acknowledged him with a gentle nod and broke the strained silence, 'We will make contact in five minutes.'

'Have you decided what you are going to say?' Dr Broom asked absently. He knew that Harry would not attempt any dealings with the Gwarks unless he was fully prepared.

'Of course. I will be firm but as friendly as possible. A respectful approach will be needed even though I would rather punch any of them in the mouth.' The last part was muttered under his breath but was clearly heard by the scientist who gaped comically at Harry.

Seeing this, Harry made a half-hearted excuse, 'Well, they have not exactly been happy to meet us half way before and the pressure is getting to me.'

'Completely understandable. I just hope we do not make matters worse.' Dr Broom admitted quietly.

Harry swiftly replied, 'I do not think that is possible, my friend.'

Just as Harry had spoken these words, the image of a female Gwark filled the screen. Her face was menacing as she stared straight into the room at the little aliens. Although silent, it was evident that she breathed heavily as her shoulders moved up and down and her chest expanded and compressed. The tusks on either side of her snout had been manicured into gleaming razor sharp points. The sides were as thin as a knife and would serve as deadly weapons. Her long mane, thick as the hair of a horse, shone from intense brushing. She lifted one large, fat hand and pointed at Harry. Her talons were long and appeared to be as solid as steel.

There was no doubt that she had often used them to kill her victims. Harry could imagine her digging them into someone's chest with the ease of a knife piercing into soft butter. This made him shiver.

'I am the Commander of the Gwark planet. You requested an meeting with me.' She boomed loudly in a gruff voice. 'What could you possibly have to say that would be of any interest to me?' She mocked and her cocky confidence was unbearable, especially to Harry who was a very proud individual.

Carefully, he composed himself not to show the rage and revulsion that he felt towards the creature on the screen. 'What I have to say is of great value to both your people and to us here on Nimara. Why do you want to start yet another battle? You were defeated by us in the last one, what makes you think you could beat us this time?'

Harry's tone sounded sarcastic in the last sentence and Dr Broom gave his companion a look to warn him against this.

'Why do you want another fight?' Harry asked again but this time using a more gentle and beseeching tone.

'You killed so many of my people; you left many of my women widowed and sonless. You killed my only son! My son!' She glared menacingly and spoke those last words with a slight emotional quiver. 'My courageous boy was slaughtered. It would have been humiliating enough if it was done by one of your pathetic soldiers but no…' She paused for breath to hide the sorrow and pain that she was feeling instead her voice changed to one full of venom and hatred. 'He was killed by a human girl who needed a pill to succeed.'

Harry exchanged a worried look with Dr Broom.

'Once my army have annihilated all of you, I personally will get hold of that girl, crush her with my bare hands and rip her into shreds. Then I will give her remains to my soldiers for their dinner. I want no trace of her existence.' She spat the words out with vehemence.

Harry winced at the violence in her words and thought of Elzbieta. He never considered the possibility of humans being the centre of the Gwarks revenge. The leader of the Gwarks was a woman who would take great pleasure in bathing in their blood.

There was no hope for a peaceful resolution that Harry hoped for but he tried one more time to reason with her by repeating, 'What makes you think that you can beat us this time?'

'You know the answer to that one already. We have your technology now and we can use it. The transporter will be most useful.' The Commander was very smug when relating this news to Harry.

'We have locked you out of the system. The transporter is of no use to you.' Harry replied with irony.

The Commander waved her hand absently as if swatting an annoying fly and answered, 'A minor setback.'

Just as she said this, Harry spotted something in the background, behind her. He was sure that he saw something moving in the shadows, hiding behind a desk. He stopped listening to her and pointed to the screen.

'What is that?' he asked, squinting his eyes in an attempt to see it more clearly. 'Who is that hiding behind the desk?'

The Commander gave an almighty booming laugh and said, 'Come out and reveal yourself. Let Harry see who is on our side now. Let him see who has abandoned his own people.'

Slowly, a large, white head emerged from under the desk. The wide, globe-like eyes darted from the Commander to the screen and seemed to focus on Harry. With a limp, he began to creep forward. His hands and feet were bound together with iron chains that pierced into his fragile wrists and ankles until they bled. He wore a simple, brown tunic that was dirty and ripped. Faded and fresh bruises covered most of his body.

Harry gaped in shock.

The alien managed to stand close enough for Harry to see him clearly, although he still kept a little distance from the female Gwark.

The alien began to speak in his native Nimaran language. This caused the Commander to reach over and grab the alien by the neck with force to pull him closer to her, 'We agreed to communicate in English during our meeting.' She threw the alien to the ground and then wiped her hands on her own clothes in disgust to remove any contamination that could be passed from him.

Getting back to his feet, the alien looked back at Harry. It was obvious how much pain he endured. Harry sadly could only feel compassion for him.

'Harry, I am so sorry.' The alien's speech was broken with emotion. He spoke with great difficulty as each word brought him pain. 'I have been a traitor to you and to our people and I feel so ashamed.'

Harry looked at his best friend and his whole heart reached out to him. 'Simon, what have you done?' There was no anger in his voice, just pity. 'We grew up together, we always did everything together, and I trusted you with my life. What have you done?' He blinked back his tears as he could only watch the broken and desperate person before him.

'I was working in the same place as the scientists when the Gwarks came to take them away. They took all of us without discrimination.' His voice was no more than a whisper and Dr Broom turned up the volume on the computer. 'I got it into my head that if I could befriend these people and teach them new skills then they would grow to like us. I sincerely believed that they would consider us their friends and leave our planet alone.'

'But look at you.' Harry regarded his friend with sorrow.

'At first they treated us well and I began to have hopes of an alliance between our two planets. How stupid I was to even think that this could be possible. Very soon after they abducted us they showed themselves for who they really were, monsters. They made me watch as they murdered all the scientists. It was horrible. The screams of pain haunt me every night.' Tears began to well up in his eyes. 'They only kept me alive because someone managed to lock the transporter. Without me, they would never be able to get it working again. If I did not unlock it then they would kill me. I was so scared.'

'So then you fixed the transporter?' Harry asked cautiously.

'I thought I did but the soldier they sent last night did not return. It is as if he disappeared into space.'

'Simon, we will get you out of this.' Harry promised.

'Are you mad with me?' Simon pleaded for some affection.

'Yes you are still my friend but just a very cowardly and stupid one.' Harry returned.

The Commander interrupted, 'So you better prepare because we are coming for you!'

With this the screen went blank. They had lost contact. Harry turned to Dr Broom but was lost for words. Dr Broom respected his silence and bowed before leaving the room.

Once he had left, Harry walked towards the window and thought of his friend, now a prisoner of the Gwarks. 'Oh Simon,' he sighed, 'You stupid fool.'

CHAPTER TWENTY FOUR

THE NEW WEAPONS

A WEEK HAD past very quickly and each day was filled with training the soldiers. Bruno was very pleased with the progress made and the soldiers seemed to be full of confidence. Each one knew what would be expected of him once a battle began.

It never ceased to amaze Bruno how diverse each talent was and how remarkable they all were. Some of the aliens could make things materialise. However, when he asked them to imagine a lethal weapon and make it appear, all that materialised was one that they already had. None of them had the imagination, creativity or violent nature to come up with anything new. He would have to rely on the scientists for this.

Bruno felt it was a shame that the meeting between Harry and the Commander was unsuccessful and was extremely concerned for Elzbieta's safety. As he was thinking about this he smiled, 'Trust her to kill the leader's son. Talk about hitting where it hurts.'

He sat on his bed and removed the wrapper from the chocolate bar that Charlie had given him the night before. Just like everything else in Nimara, the chocolate was so much richer and creamier than at home. When the time would come to leave Nimara, he planned to take some bars with him if he was allowed to so. The Nimaran people did not want too many humans knowing about their existence. They grew to trust the few select individuals but still feared the Earth people as a whole. Besides, how could he explain where he got the chocolate from to his parents? That would be impossible.

While deep in thought and eating the smooth chocolate there was a knock on the door and Charlie poked his head in, 'Bruno, Harry will not like it if you are late.'

'I know. I'm just coming.' Bruno replied and threw the wrapper into the bin and reached for his trainers. He was due to have a meeting with Harry and he hoped to be updated on what the scientists had been working on. So far he was kept in the dark and had no idea about their progress with inventing new weapons or medicines. Now, would be the right time to have some information as he was ready to take the next step with his army, although he was not quite sure what this would be be.

Rushing out of the apartment and out of the front door of the building, Bruno dodged past the aliens that were in his way. He was curious to know what Harry had to report to him and so he sprinted all the way back to the huge building in the middle of the city. Once inside, he dashed towards Harry's office door and paused for breath before entering.

'Ah, there you are. Take a seat please.' Harry gestured towards the chair opposite his own. As Bruno settled into the seat, Harry did the same and placed his hands together on the table between them. He wore a serious expression and this made Bruno nervous. Squirming in his seat, he remembered the last time he had seen that exact expression on Harry's face. It was when he was about to be told about the pill, the one he was expected to take during the battle, in order to change into an alien. Of course, this did not happen, due to Elzbieta's intervention, but he was fully aware of the pain that she had suffered when taking it herself.

'I have lots of things to tell you.' Harry began. 'Firstly, Dr Gaton assures me that they are very close to creating a serum that heals wounds within seconds. In fact, if used quickly enough, it has the power to regenerate lost limbs in perfect working order. On top of this, they have been working on a lotion that once applied to the body will harden the skin. It will prevent any injury or pain to our soldiers caused through weapons or punches during a battle. In fact, they believe that it works so well that it protects against a blast from a flame thrower. The lotion should last about five days which should be ample time.'

Stunned by this information Bruno replied, 'It all sounds amazing but war can last for years. I know we won it in a day last time but who is to say this one will not last more than five days?'

Harry impatiently replied, 'No battle in our solar system has ever lasted more than three days let alone five,' He clearly had more exciting information to tell Bruno. 'Dr Hallon has told me that Dr Stenner himself worked diligently on a weapon that is far more sophisticated than any created before. A gun that is no bigger than a disc, fitted into the palm of the hand. The devise will be fused into the flesh and controlled mentally.'

Bruno's eyes widened and he sat up straight in his seat, raising his voice in panic said, 'Hold on there, are you saying that you need to cut out a round hole in the palm of a hand and then fit a disc into it?'

Harry answered very matter of fact, 'The operation will be painless, I can guarantee that. You humans will have temporary ones. After the battle it will be removed again. You cannot go home with such a weapon, you must understand that.'

Bruno's mouth fell open at the mere thought of it and asked with a shaky voice, 'and be left with a hole in the hand? Can't we just have the old guns and leave the new ones to the soldiers?' He felt the heat rush to his face and his heart drumming in his chest.

'Don't be silly,' Harry laughed, 'I can imagine your concern but we do have medicines that heal those kind of wounds. We can manipulate the molecule structure of the skin and flesh so that...' waving his hand in the air, he decided not to get too complicated as Bruno would not understand anyway. 'Suffice to say, it is not a problem. The only thing that will be a problem is linking the device to your brainwaves. Your patterns are less sophisticated than ours and you do not use them to the same capacity. So, all of you will have to take the pill.'

'I don't think I could go through with that. You know what happened last time.' Bruno felt ashamed to admit that he was afraid to take the pill.

Harry reassuringly replied, 'yes, but this time you know it works. We have perfected it and it is now utterly painless. The transformation is smoother and quicker.'

Wanting to hear nothing more about the pill, Bruno changed the subject, 'so, what do you want me to do?'

Harry sat back in his chair and folded his arms, 'we need to test the serum and lotion. Can you select ten soldiers to do this? Nine Nimarans and one human. We must make sure it works on both types of people.'

Bruno's face became white, 'you are not going to chop anyone's leg or arm off are you?' He dared to ask.

'No, I think we will just have to risk it and hope it can actually heal. Let's just hope it works.'

Bruno sighed with relief.

'So, who do you want to be experimented on?' Harry prompted and raised an eyebrow to show he wanted a response.

Bruno thought for a few moments and then responded, 'I will choose the nine Nimarans at random. However, I cannot allow anything to happen to Summer and Elzbieta has already given so much of herself that it would be wrong to even suggest using her again. Greg is the new addition to the group and I feel that he will be the prefect selection for the experiment.'

Harry's face dropped and he pursed his thin lips tightly together as though he was displeased with the choice but decided not to say anything.

Bruno's face burned and developed a pink hue. He was embarrassed by not putting himself forward for the test and proving himself the hero. However, he was truly frightened of what could go wrong. He averted his eyes away from Harry and lowered his head.

'Very well,' Harry's tone was sharp and unforgiving. He then continued, 'You must tell the chosen ones to come here at dawn tomorrow. The sooner we find out if the serum and lotion works, the better.' Harry raised himself from his seat slowly and grimaced. Bruno noticed that Harry had aged in the past two years and at times he reminded him of Granddad. When he made this comparison, he brushed it away as it made him feel uneasy. Harry was the eternal voice of power and leadership. Any visible weakness made him seem vulnerable and not the right kind of image for a leader in Bruno's eyes.

Bruno stood up and still avoiding any eye contact with Harry, quietly muttered, 'I will go and tell the chosen ones now.'

As Bruno reached the door, Harry called out, 'Bruno.'

Bruno stopped but did not turn around.

In a more gentle voice Harry continued, 'tell Greg first; he deserves that much.'

For a few seconds, Bruno closed his eyes and remained completely still. His hands were clenched at his sides. His heart raced in his chest. Telling Greg that he had been chosen to be experimented on was not going to be easy. In his mind, he could picture Greg's eyes widen in fear. He sighed heavily and then opened the door.

CHAPTER TWENTY FIVE

BRUNO BREAKS THE NEWS

BY THE TIME Bruno returned to Charlie's apartment, it was late afternoon. He could not force himself to go straight to see Greg to break the news as he had promised Harry. Instead he found himself roaming the streets of the city, barely focusing on anything that was going on around him. When he returned to Charlie's flat, he could clearly hear that Summer, Elzbieta and Charlie were in the Dragon's room.

Charlie was fussing about the amount of food that the dragon was eating.

'I don't want Herbert to get fat! Please stop giving him so many treats. It is just not good for him.' Charlie's frantic voice echoed down the corridor as Bruno quietly closed the front door. He stood still and continued to listen. The two girls giggled, evidently dismissing Charlie's concern.

The flat always felt welcoming and Bruno would normally smile to himself when he heard the sounds of laughter or just the general day to day conversation between his friends. On this occasion he felt nothing but shame and a sense of dread. He knew that his friends would abhor him for his decision.

As if walking to his doom, he slowly moved towards them, his face grew paler with every step he took. His throat felt thick with the taste of bile and he swallowed hard to keep it down.

When he reached the doorway he watched the action that was taking place inside the room. The two girls were stroking Herbert who looked very content with all the attention he was getting. Charlie had his face buried in one of the sacks of food which looked ridiculously comical.

After a little while Charlie lifted his head and pouted at the two girls and said, 'I am going to have to buy some more now. It is expensive you know.'

Elzbieta looked at him and smiled. Her amusement was visible in her shining eyes as she said, 'Charlie, I will go and get some more for you.'

'That is not the point, it is me who will have to pay for it. Besides, Herbert needs to be kept on a strict diet.'

Summer watched Charlie whilst tickling Herbert under the chin. The dragon had now placed his head gently on her left arm and his long tail was curled around her feet. Wisps of smoke puffed from his nostrils as he took deep and slow breaths.

She had been alerted by something in the corner of her eye and she suddenly turned her attention to the doorway. Her smile dropped when she saw Bruno lurking there, so silent and still.

'Bruno...' her voice was soft and full of concern.

Elzbieta and Charlie turned towards the doorway, distracted from their conversation.

'Where have you been?' Summer asked cautiously.

Bruno merely glanced at the three faces before him and leaned his head against the doorframe. The others waited for a response patiently. It was obvious that Bruno had something bad to tell them.

'Is Greg here?' Bruno whispered shakily.

Charlie bewilderingly replied, 'Yes, in his room.'

'Can you go and get him please? I want all of you to go to the lounge. We need to talk.' Before Bruno finished his sentence, he already began to move away from the others and trudged down the corridor towards the lounge.

The three of them remained silent and stared at each other anxiously.

'I will go and get Greg now,' Charlie announced and swiftly left the room.

★

Bruno waited for the others to enter the room. So many thoughts raced around in his mind. How was he going to break the news to them, to Greg? What damage would this cause to their relationship with him? Would Summer no longer respect him? What bothered him the most was that even though he felt guilty and ashamed, he still lacked the courage to volunteer.

In single file the others entered the room. Each one looked at Bruno with a mixture of fear, concern and confusion but no one said a word. Quickly they took their seats around the coffee table.

Bruno began to speak with his head bent down, staring at his clasped hands that shook nervously on his lap, 'I really do not know where to start.'

Summer leaned forward and took hold of Bruno's hands and smiled sincerely at him and said, 'At the beginning.'

The touch of her warm, soft hands and the sheer love reflected in her countenance caused him to crumble. A tear slipped down his face. Nodding, Bruno took a deep breath and started to talk. He told them about the wonderful inventions and how the scientists had progressed so quickly. His audience were captivated even though they waited in anticipation for the news that had obviously distressed him.

For the three humans, the whole concept of each invention was beyond the realms of possibility and in fact more creative than any dreamt up by science fiction writers. Even Charlie gasped in awe and clapped his hands excitedly.

'Now, these inventions are at the stage where they need to be tested,' Bruno had now got to the point that he tried to put off for as long as possible. 'We need to choose nine Nimarans to be experimented on.'

Charlie looked nervous and interrupted Bruno by asking, 'But is it safe? I don't want anyone to get hurt.'

Bruno, due to his own problem, had not given any thought or consideration to the fact that Charlie would naturally have concerns for his own people.

'We will choose nine soldiers at random,' he continued, ignoring Charlie's intrusion. 'There was also a request for one human.' He paused to assess the reaction of his friends but they all stared blankly at him.

'I have told Harry that Greg will be the person that will be tested on. He has assured me that nothing would go wrong and that no limbs would be chopped off...

damn!' As soon as the words leapt out of his mouth, he realised how bad they sounded.

Greg sat in stunned silence trying to let the situation sink in. His mouth was open and his tongue was pressed tightly to the roof of his mouth.

Elzbieta snapped angrily, 'Why Greg? Why not me or you for that matter?'

Before Bruno could give an answer, Greg intercepted. The simple words that he spoke caused Bruno's heart to finally smash into a million pieces.

'I guess I am the most imperfect one here. I need help to be stronger. When does the experiment begin?'

CHAPTER TWENTY SIX

DAWN ARRIVES TOO SOON

GREG ROSE EARLY as he did most mornings, just before dawn and raced to the top of the hill that overlooked the city. Once he reached his perfect spot, he collapsed onto his back and waited for dawn to break. Greg was so mesmerised by the whole display that he could not help himself but to say in a loud voice, full of emotion, 'Dawn in Nimara is the most beautiful sight that anyone could ever be fortunate enough to experience.'

Every evening he found himself becoming more and more excited and could not wait for the next day to arrive. He had not told anyone about his morning adventures as it was his little secret that he wanted to keep for himself. It sometimes made him chuckle to think that this was his addiction, the bright colours of dawn. At least it was safer and more exhilarating than any hallucination induced through drugs.

After a short while of watching the splendour, he realised that this time it was a totally different experience for him. With a heavy heart and sadness he watched the pastel shaded blasts of fire that exploded like glitter coated fireworks with the thought that this could possibly be the last time that he would see all this.

He had accepted every single situation thrown at him since stepping on Nimara. He took it all as a wonderful adventure and truly believed that he would return safely home to his mum. Not even for a moment did he think that his life could actually be in danger, even when the Gwark got uncomfortably close to him. He was frightened but still trusted that he would be fine.

This time, however, he was not so sure. He would be experimented on and no-one really knew what the outcome would be.

Suddenly a loud boom echoed across the sky and vibrated over the hills. It always reminded him of the roll of a base drum that he once heard in an orchestra when the performance was about to begin. It was his favourite part of the show.

The clouds appeared to gather together and form a perfectly choreographed sequence dance as a back drop of intermittent flashing lights across the sky. In short intervals the lights changed colour from blue to green to purple and then red, orange and silver. Glitter was dropped down as if by the angels in heaven and tongues of fire licked at the clouds as they danced and sang joyfully. All this lasted for about five minutes until the two suns joined the three moons to watch over the planet.

Once this was over, Greg knew that he must go to see Harry and let fate lead him to whatever awaited him.

★

Greg stood in Harry's office along with the nine chosen Nimaran soldiers. All of them looked just as nervous as he was. Some stood very still with hands clenched tightly that each knuckle was white from the strain. Others shook and whimpered. Greg just gaped at the others around him and from time to time wiped away the moisture from his eyes. He was determined not to cry.

Harry stood behind his desk and observed all nine aliens and Greg. Whenever his eyes met Greg's his face became etched with pain and pity.

After a few moments the door opened and Dr Hallon and Dr Stenner entered. Dr. Hallon beamed with enthusiasm and looked at the aliens one by one. She then stopped in front of Greg and her smile dropped. She opened her mouth as if she was going to say something, paused and as if thinking better of it, she closed it again and tried to smile at him.

Dr Stenner merely grunted and sat on the edge of Harry's desk. He was not interested with the subjects before him. All he cared about was the outcome of the experiments. So much work had gone into the development of the weapons and lotion; it had to work.

Harry motioned Dr Hallon to speak. She nodded and took her place directly in front of Harry's desk and faced the ten subjects. She cleared her throat and began, 'Today, all of you are part of a very exciting experiment. We believe that we have perfected the most effective weapon ever to have been designed. You are the lucky chosen few who will be the first to have this weapon installed. After installation is complete, we will begin to train you on how to use it. This should be accomplished by the end of the day. For the next stage of the experiment you will all be kept under observation for a day after we apply a serum all over your bodies. Once it takes effect, then a series of tests will be executed in order to give us an insight of how effective it really is. There will be physical changes for you to get used to and a psychologist will be made available at any time whilst you are in our care.' She paused and in a tone that suggested uncertainty proclaimed. 'You will not be in any pain at any stage of the process. There may be slight discomfort at times but nothing more.'

After Dr Hallon finished speaking, Greg noticed Harry lower his head. It was evident that even he was not at all sure whether this was a good idea.

Dr Stenner made a deep, rumbling noise as he cleared his throat, 'I believe it's time to get on with it.' He looked at Dr Hallon impatiently and his lower lip protruded as he pouted angrily.

'Yes, quite right,' Dr Hallon clapped her hands together eagerly. 'We have much to do. We will escort you all to the Laboratory where our assistants will bath you and give you gowns to wear. Everything must be perfectly sterile. We want to avoid any chance of infections occurring. The process of installing the weapon into the palm of your hand will be explained in detail. Once we are ready to proceed, we will deal with you one by one.'

At this point Harry raised his hand as a sign that he had something to say. 'In front of me I see brave men and courageous soldiers. My admiration for you knows no bounds. Good luck my friends.' Although looking strained and exhausted he clutched the table for support and remained standing as they were led out of the room.

All the way to the Laboratory, Greg felt it was all a dream and that this was not really happening. His head felt light and his legs barely carried him forward to his destination. He could feel the blood pulse within his veins and his mouth had gone dry. Still feeling hazy, he allowed the assistant to pour water over his body and then rub a strong disinfectant all over it. This was done in total silence and Greg refused to even look at the alien who was washing him. He had let his thoughts wander back home to the time when he used to stand and wave to the children going off to school. That was the time that he felt most safe and wished more than anything in the world that he could now run into the arms of his mother. She would hold him tightly and shield him from any harm.

Whilst the scientists explained how the small gun would be fitted into the palm of the hand, depending on whether the subject was left or right handed, Greg barely listened. He did not want to know what they were going to do until it was all over.

Being the only human there, the scientists decided to take him in first. Greg was relieved not to be sitting out in the corridor with the other aliens… waiting.

Dr Stenner and Dr Hallon were already dressed, ready for the operation to be performed. They had masks over their faces but there movements were instantly recognisable. Another alien was in the room and she smiled sweetly at Greg and assured him that everything would be absolutely fine. She touched his forehead gently and Greg instantly felt dizzy. His eyes became heavy and then there was nothing.

'Greg, Greg wake up dear.'

Greg's lids felt glued shut and he felt as if he was being called from somewhere far away. He could feel a soft, tingling sensation across his forehead.

'Greg it's over, you can wake up now.'

Slowly, Greg prised his lids apart and was met by yet another nurse who was smiling at him. She took her hand away from his forehead and explained, 'It was a success. We were worried that your body would reject a foreign object but it is already healing very well.'

Greg immediately picked up his right hand towards his eyes and saw a large bandage covering it. Specks of blood had seeped through and his palm was very itchy and slightly sore.

'Try not to move it too much at the moment. We will bathe it in an hour and you should be able to use the gun by this afternoon. Of course, it will still feel a little sore but you will be well on the way to recovery.'

Greg still felt sleepy and allowed himself to drift off into a deep and calm slumber.

When he woke up he felt completely refreshed and his hand no longer itched. When he lifted it, he found that it was heavier than the other one and automatically looked at it. He gasped in disbelief. His hand no longer had the lines that ran across his palm; they had been replaced with a smooth, dense metal disk of about 2 inches in diameter. The wound around the disk was red but his skin appeared to have moulded itself around the disk, holding it firmly in place and blending in as part of his hand. He examined the top of his hand and although the colour of his skin was slightly a darker shade where the disk sat, it could not be clearly seen through it. It must have sat just below a thin layer of flesh and skin. His bones and veins in his hand were still in the right place. Greg was fascinated and could not tare his eyes away from it.

The nurse who woke him up earlier entered the room and smiled when she saw him sitting up in the bed. She placed a tray on the side table and then took the lid off that was covering one of the plates. The room instantly smelled of roast chicken and gravy. To Greg's surprise his stomach began growling loudly like a vicious dog. He was feeling very hungry. The nurse also brought a large glass of lemonade and Greg watched the ice tinkle around the sides of the glass and the bubbles pop excitedly as they leapt in the air. The straw bopped but stayed in the glass.

'After you have satisfied your hunger and thirst, you will meet with the others in the laboratory. We now have to connect your brain to the weapon for it to work.' She handed the lemonade to Greg and watched as he took several long sips through the straw. 'You have been through the worse bit, I promise you. The next stage will be to re-educate your thought patterns to adjust to the need to control an added element to your body. Once this has been done, then the fun begins and you get to practice using the gun.

After saying this, the nurse started to move towards the door. She swiftly turned back to Greg and pointing towards the food announced with a big smile, 'Enjoy!' Turning back to the door, she left.

CHAPTER TWENTY SEVEN

BRAINWAVES

IT WAS TIME for the second stage of the experiment and Greg found himself once more in the laboratory with the nine aliens. The air was still thick with anticipation but the icy chill of fear had vanished. Instead, there was a sense of calm and a little excitement that rumbled through their whispered conversations. Greg listened to the high pitched ramblings of the aliens that still hurt his ears.

He noticed that the room had been re-arranged in order to accommodate ten beds that were placed in a row. Next to each bed was a metal device that was shaped like a hood. It reminded Greg of the old hair dryers once used in a hair salon. He had seen them on the website. By each bed was an alien who stood very still and looked extremely serious. Their brilliant white, creaseless gowns hung loosely around them. They wore green rubber gloves that fit tightly into their skin all the way up to their elbows and wore a mask over their face. Greg was surprised that Dr

Hallon and Dr Stenner were absent. He thought that they would want to oversee every stage of the process. The formal setting and behaviour of the nurses made Greg feel very uncomfortable. He remembered the kind nurse who brought him food and told him that there would be no pain in this part of the test. How could she possibly know that when no-one else did? This was a new situation for both human and alien alike.

The nurse closest to Greg beckoned him towards the bed and he reluctantly moved towards her. Simultaneously, all of the aliens stopped whispering to each other and took their places by the bed designated to them. The silence was a monster that crept through the room, crawling up each victim's back clawing at their spines as it moved along.

The nurse gently pushed Greg down on the bed until he settled into a more comfortable position. The hood was positioned above his face and when Greg peered inside he could see small colourful lights swirl around. Looking at them made him feel disorientated and slightly nauseous.

The nurse gazed down at him and quietly said, 'Do try to relax. It will be easier for you if you do. Let your thoughts drift away.'

This almost made Greg laugh as it was impossible to do what she asked as a multitude of thoughts filled his mind; all wanting to push their way to the front.

Suddenly the lights became very bright and stung his eyes. He tried to shut them but found it difficult. Then, he could hear a high pitched whine as if the machine was moaning. The noise inside his head became unbearable and painful. It felt as if his head would explode. This lasted for about five minutes and yet it felt like hours. When the hood was finally removed his tense body relaxed and his muscles ached. He was covered in sweat yet he was shivering with cold. Greg felt dazed and confused, and found it difficult to speak. He tried very hard to open and shut his mouth but the words simply would not come out.

The nurse hovered over him and wiped his forehead with a flannel and spoke reassuringly, 'You must rest for a while. Then you will feel absolutely fine.'

She brushed her hand over his brow and Greg fell into a deep sleep.

★

Greg opened his eyes and sat up. He felt no pain at all. He shook his head and found that he did not even have a headache. He felt strangely refreshed considering what he had been through. Looking around, he saw that he was in the same room and that the other aliens were also waking up. Some were smiling with relief whilst others looked bewildered, as they rubbed their heads.

The nurses placed their clothes in a neat pile next to them, ready for them to put on. Greg was more than happy to shed the gown that he was wearing.

Once they were all ready to leave, they were told to make their way to the amphitheatre.

As they strolled through the corridors, Greg could feel a change in the attitude of the group. Instead of negative emotions, which would have been quite normal under the circumstances seeing what they went through, there was an enthusiastic buzz. This could be attributed to the worst part of their ordeal being over. Greg did not hold a grudge towards the aliens or in fact towards Bruno and felt a lot happier now about the whole experience. He knew that by overcoming fear, pain and the injustice of being selected for the experiment meant that he survived as a good and stronger human being.

They all soon reached the amphitheatre and descended the stairs towards the stage were Dr Hallon and Dr Stenner were waiting for them. Once they all settled in their seats, Dr Hallon stepped forward with Dr Stenner remaining behind her, grumbling to himself before fishing around in his pocket and pulling out a very large biscuit. He studied the biscuit from all angles and then shoved it all into his mouth. As he crammed it in, crumbs exploded from the sides of his mouth and catapulted to the floor.

Ignoring the strange grunts and crunching noises going on behind her, Dr Hallon addressed her audience. 'All of you have gone through a gruelling time and achieved it with success. The whole process so far has gone better than expected.' She paused and smiled nervously. 'Now, we will find out if all our labours are fruitful. We will see if you can control the guns. I must stress that this must be done very carefully. What you have been fitted with is a highly advanced laser gun. It can only be controlled through brainpower. This means each of you must learn to control any murderous thoughts towards anyone except your enemy.' When she said this she turned and stared at Greg, who had begun to blush. He hated being singled out. 'When you make your first attempts to use the gun, you must make sure that you do not face anyone directly. This may seem obvious but I just want it to be absolutely clear.

You are responsible for a highly dangerous weapon. In fact you are the highly dangerous weapon. Now, find your own space in this room and remember to face away from any other person.'

All ten of them did as instructed immediately and waited in their chosen areas. They all decided to face the wall.

Dr Hallon continued, 'Close your eyes and breathe deeply. Clear your minds of any thoughts and concentrate purely on the disc in the palm of your hand. Feel its weight, feel how cool it makes your skin surrounding it. Imagine a button that you can press, visualise that button in your mind. Think what it looks like. The colour, its shape, is it round or square?'

Greg concentrated firmly on all of this and could clearly see a red button on a round, black base.

Once Dr Hallon was certain that they all understood and were ready she said, 'Press the button,'

As soon as the words tumbled out of her mouth, Greg's hand opened wide and his finger touched the imaginary button when a surging force shot out from the middle of his palm. It pulled his arm in different directions and Greg stared at the beam of orange light that flew out. It made a gaping hole in the wall before him and as its force controlled his arm, he swung around and five of the other aliens had to duck to avoid being shot. Whatever the beam touched exploded or merely vanished.

Dr Hallon shouted, 'Press that button again. Press — that — button!'

Greg managed to visualise the button again and saw the same finger press it down. Instantly, the beam stopped and he was left panting with exhaustion. His arm was sore from being yanked around but the palm of his hand felt no different. The laser did not affect him in any way. Looking around he saw the extent of the damage that he had caused and watched as the five aliens slowly stood up straight, their faces etched with panic.

Dr Hallon sighed heavily, 'I think we should perhaps do this outside and prepare a target in the form of a Gwark for you to aim at.'

Dr Stenner merely grunted in agreement.

'Did you notice that the human managed to use the weapon, even though he did not take the pill?' Dr Hallon whispered to her companion. 'I thought they would have to become one of us for them to function the weapon.'

Dr Stenner however was not so surprised, 'Remember, this boy has a far more superior brain to the rest of the humans. He is highly imaginative.' Turning to face Dr Hallon he remarked, 'Don't expect so much from the others, they will need the pill.'

The nine aliens and Greg were kept in a nearby dormitory and were told that they could not return to their homes until the experiments were complete.

Greg had a room to himself as he was the only human and after he wrecked the amphitheatre almost killing the aliens in the process, they were too scared to go near him. Their fear of him continued even though he proved after more practice that he could control the laser safely. This did not bother him however, as, to be truthful, Greg preferred to be alone. So much had happened to him that he needed time to gather his thoughts together.

Lying on the bed with only the dimming light of day to see by, he stared at his hand. He did not believe that he could ever get used to the object that had been inserted into his palm. Yet, the conflicting thought of how amazing it was stirred excitement within him. Other boys could only imagine, in their most creative of dreams, something like this happening to them. He was a lethal weapon and he liked the sound of that.

Slowly, he drifted off to sleep wondering what the next day had in store for him.

CHAPTER TWENTY EIGHT

THE LOTION

THE NEXT MORNING the alarm bellowed through the dormitory like a raging banshee. It tore through the corridors and whirled around each room, forcing the aliens and Greg to wake up abruptly. Greg winced at the noise and automatically covered his ears. Remembering the weapon in his hand he quickly withdrew it. He felt confident that he could control it but did not want to take any risks.

After quickly getting changed and following the other nine aliens across the corridor to the laboratory, Greg felt light headed and rather queasy. It seemed to be one of the traits of the Nimaran people to unveil information little by little. From one moment to the next he was never sure what was going to happen. At times the element of surprise was thrilling but at others, it caused him to feel physically sick with worry. This was yet another one of those times.

Dr Stenner and Dr Hallon were waiting for their subjects for further testing and watched patiently as they entered into the room.

Dr Stenner was the first to greet them this time. He waddled forward, grunting and muttering as he did so. He had only taken a few steps forward and yet his gestures were dramatic and slow. With a final long and rumbling groan that resonated from the back of his throat he began to speak, 'We will be moving on to the next experiment. A lotion has been created that will prevent anything from hurting you. In fact, we firmly believe that even the laser from your hand will not penetrate your skin and you are all aware of how powerful it is.' He smiled smugly, distorting his features and giving him an appearance of insanity. 'The lotion will be rubbed into your skin. After this we will test its strength. Your skin will harden and feel extremely dry but apart from that there should be no other effects.'

Dr Hallon stepped forward; her smile was more genuine and said, 'The tests will be gradual by starting with mild physical attacks. If these prove successful and do not hurt you any way then we will move onto guns, swords and finally bombs. We may consider using your lasers but that is still a matter to be discussed.' She glared coldly at Dr Stenner as she said this. He chose to ignore her and merely circled his eyes.

To Greg's astonishment, instead of a nurse entering the room to smear the lotion on each of them, Dr Hallon simply handed out a large, heavy pot to each individual. When Greg received his, he held it up to his face and moved the pot around slowly. The substance was pastel pink and did not easily slide out from its container. It was obviously thick and gloopy.

'Remember,' Dr Hallon continued, 'You must rub the lotion all over your body and not miss any area at all. Not one inch of you should be left exposed.'

'No Achilles heel,' Greg whispered to himself. He had always loved to listen to his mother tell the story of Achilles who was dipped in the river Styx by his mother Thetis because it offered powers of invulnerability to prevent death. She held him by the heel which prevented it from being touched by the magical river. One day a poisonous arrow shot at him was lodged in his heel, killing him shortly after. 'Definitely, no Achilles heel.' Greg's eyes widened at the thought of having bombs blasted at him.

When Dr Hallon finished her instructions they were all sent back to their rooms to shower, dry and then apply the lotion. Greg slowly opened the pot and sniffed it. There was no scent at all. Gingerly, he dipped his fingers into the jar and let the lotion cover them. The substance was ice cold and very dense. It reminded him of a sticky marshmallow that he once tried that stuck to the roof of his mouth. Of course he would not be eating this concoction, but the thought of smearing it over his entire body made him cringe.

Bravely, he dug his whole hand in and yanked it out without hesitation and smacked it down onto his arm. Instead of sticking, it glided smoothly and seeped into his skin. Greg began to relax as it was not as bad as he thought it would be. Carefully, he rubbed it everywhere, even into his scalp. He was not going to leave any spot vulnerable to attack.

★

After they applied the lotion and let it set for an hour, the rest of the day was filled with intensive training. Using the laser had become second nature and Greg almost subconsciously envisaged the button that made the disk in his palm work. He gained complete control of his weapon and found that he had become very skilful.

It was very difficult to sleep that night because the lotion made his skin intolerably itchy. When he moved, he noticed that a whole layer of skin was lying on his bed. He felt like a snake shedding his skin and was revolted by the fact that he had to pick it up and place it in the bin. On top of that, the underneath layer was solid and reminded him of a lizard he had stroked in a zoo. He shivered at the thought.

It was early morning and Greg sat on his bed after having a restless night. He dreaded what the day would bring as it was now time to test how well the lotion worked. He wondered what tests would be done and at what point would the doctors feel that enough was enough. Would they really make the aliens and himself fight against each other with the lasers? Could they be so sure that the lotion was that effective? This was a very disturbing and frightening thought.

CHAPTER TWENTY NINE

IT WORKS!

'IT WORKS', DR Hallon gasped, 'It really does work.' Her eyes were wide with astonishment as she watched the nine aliens and the human launch streams of light from the palms of their hands at each other. The display was magnificent and blasts of green, yellow, red and blue flashed furiously left and right. When the beam of light met one of the soldiers it did not bounce off or burst into flames, it merely just stopped. The hardened skin that it touched appeared to extinguish the laser. The sophisticated weapons that they were using seemed so useless, only when a target was missed and the laser hit a tree, a rock or even the ground could the true extent of its power be seen. There were large craters in the field, the rocks smashed into pieces and trees crumbled to ash. The soldiers were highly energetic and flew across the air and moved with such speed that at times they were just blurred figures. All of them were laughing with joy as though they were in fact, just having a harmless snowball fight. They were invincible – the lotion was a complete success.

'Marvellous,' Harry rocked excitedly on his feet and clapped his hands together, 'You have achieved some wondrous inventions. I am in awe of your talents.'

Dr Hallon grinned with pride whilst Dr Stenner grunted to himself. Nothing seemed to excite him. He then cleared his throat and said, 'I would like to test the serum.'

Harry clearly showed that he was not happy with the suggestion replied, 'There will not be any limbs cut off. We will have to trust that the serum works.' After a short pause Harry asked, 'Are you ready to fit the rest of the soldiers with the weapon and get them to apply the lotion?'

'Yes,' Dr Stenner answered. 'We would like to start with the humans first as they may take a little longer to adapt. Greg is an exceptional individual and his mind is strong and creative. I do not believe the others are so adaptable.'

'We will need to have the pill ready as I am convinced that they will need it to work the weapon.' Dr Hallon added.

Harry nodded thoughtfully, 'Very well, I will have one of my team give you a large supply of them. The sooner everyone is ready, the sooner we can send them to fight. Time is running out and The Gwarks could be here at any moment.'

No sooner had his words left his mouth he heard Rose frantically calling him. He turned to see her running towards him, red faced with panic and waving a wok around wildly as she stumbled once or twice. Her normally neat hair was in disarray. She finally reached the spot where Harry and the others were standing and took a moment to catch her breath.

'Oh my goodness… really… oh my!' she panted.

The others watched her. Harry noticed that the wok still had strings of noodles stuck to the base and there were chunks of carrots and runner beans glued to the sides, coated with a dark sauce. As Rose swung the wok around the noodles became unstuck and flew out, landing flatly on the grass by her toes.

'A Gwark suddenly appeared in my kitchen.' She cried. 'He was holding an axe and came charging up to me.'

Harry looked stunned, 'What did you do?'

'I wacked him with my wok.' Rose answered rather matter of fact and swung it across her body to demonstrate.

'What happened then?' Harry asked. Concern was evident with the expression on his face.

'He disappeared.' Rose smiled triumphantly.

'Could you be specific? I need to know exactly how he disappeared.' Harry urged.

'Ok,' Rose sighed, 'I wacked him across the head like this…' Taking a couple of paces away from the others, she held the wok high over her head and then brought it sharply down as if hitting a tall object. 'He seemed surprised and a bit dazed and then pressed something on his wrist and he just disappeared.'

'He pressed something?' Harry pounced on that comment quickly and pressed his lips tightly together. 'Hmm… a signal to transport him back. Once he returned, the Gwarks would know that the transporter does in fact work. Harry bowed his head in grief, 'Oh Simon, what have they made you do now?'

'That means we will have to work fast.' Dr Hallon said determinedly. 'Harry, get the humans to go to the lab now. There is no time to waste.'

'Yes, of course. You are absolutely right.' Harry whispered, his thoughts were still on his friend who was still under the control of the Gwarks. 'I will send Greg to get them. At least they will see the success of the experiment.'

CHAPTER THIRTY

THE TRUTH IS TOLD

BRUNO PRODDED GREG from every angle. The feel of the tough, leathery skin made him frown. It felt dry to the touch and as he pushed his finger into the flesh it crinkled but remained firm. Even Greg's hair had become wiry and dry, making it stand up as though a lot of hairspray had been used. Slowly, he placed the palm of his hand on the top of Greg's hair and felt each strand prick his skin like a needle.

Through all of this, Greg remained still and let Bruno explore the changes to him that had taken place. He knew what pain and discomfort his friends would have to endure in the process and was not sure if he should tell them the whole truth. He could see the fear in all of their eyes and even Charlie looked uncertain.

'Harry wants you to go to the lab… now,' he informed them.

Charlie was automatically about to obey the command as he always did but Greg stopped him,

'Harry said it was just the humans. I think you should stay here Charlie.'

Charlie looked up at Greg in surprise and then shifted back to where he had originally stood, right by Bruno's side. Disappointment flickered over his face but then changed to one of sheer relief.

'Show me your hand?' Bruno asked quietly.

Greg lifted his hand, with the palm facing up to Bruno. He knew that he had total control over the device and was confident that Bruno was completely safe even at this close proximity. Bruno appeared to trust Greg as he did not even flinch from it. In fact he studied it closely, seeing how it fit inside his hand.

'Did it hurt?' he asked meekly.

Greg dreaded this question and decided to tell half-truths, 'No, I was asleep when they fitted it in and when I woke it just itched. He paused and looked at each pair of eyes that willed him to assure them that everything was going to be fine. He continued, 'It looks worse than what it is. The aliens make it as comfortable as possible. Trust me.'

'What happened over the last two days?' Summer asked.

'On the first day they fitted the laser gun into my hand and in the afternoon they fiddled with my brain so that I could use the weapon.' He rushed through this to prevent them from asking more detailed questions. There was no way that he could let them know about the excruciating pain that he went through in the lab. 'I then began to learn how to use the weapon. On the following day I was monitored after applying the lotion and then went through more training until I was able to skilfully use the gun. It was all accomplished very quickly.'

'You make it sound as though you enjoyed the experience.' Summer commented rather sarcastically.

'Actually, in some ways I did, especially when we practiced using the laser guns.' He smiled broadly as if to confirm his enthusiasm.

'Greg, how did Harry act when he spoke to you?' Bruno frowned.

Greg thought about this for a moment and replied, 'Distracted and frustrated... he had just been speaking to Rose who was swinging a wok around and talking in wild panic.'

Bruno raised his eyebrow, 'There must be new developments that we don't know about.'

'I guess after they fix us with the laser guns and lotion we will be going to the Gwarks' planet to fight them.' Elzbieta announced thoughtfully.

Bruno spun round and looked at Elzbieta. His face softened as he regarded the determined expression worn by his friend.

'Elzbieta, I have been meaning to tell you something.' He began and then stopped. He was not sure how to proceed. How could he tell her that she was in great danger as the leader of the Gwarks was hell-bent on killing her? In a split second he decided another tactic and hoped that it would suffice. 'I don't want you to go to the planet. We need some best soldiers to stay back here.'

Elzbieta's eyes grew wide and her mouth fell open in disbelief, 'You want me to stay here?' She fired back at him, 'You can't split us up; we are a team. We fight together.'

Summer immediately joined in with the argument, 'That's right Bruno, what are you thinking of? We all fight as a team, it's how we work.'

Bruno understood the girls' reaction but felt at a loss of how to explain his reasons for this decision. 'I need someone strong and reliable to take control here.' He made a vague attempt to reason with them.

'You are not telling us something,' Elzbieta said suspiciously. 'There must be something behind all this, you don't make decisions like that.' Her eyes bore into his and Bruno was forced to look away.

Sighing he gave up the fight and realised that the truth was the only way to resolve this, 'You know when we last fought the Gwarks and you took the pill?'

Both Elzbieta and Summer listened intently and nodded at the same time.

'Remember how you killed quite a few Gwarks as you swooped down and bombarded them? Well, one of them happened to be the Commanders son. She wants your blood.' He gave a lop-sided grimace. 'That's why I want you to stay here. It will be safer.'

Silence had crept in and filled the room. All five of them stood still, Bruno looking sheepishly at his feet, Elzbieta and Summer were stunned, Charlie held his hands over his face and was shaking with fear for Elzbieta's safety and Greg just watched what everyone else was doing.

After a few moments Elzbieta broke the silence, 'You think leaving me here will keep me safe?' she replied, her voice low and calm. 'Do you not think that when the Commander realises where I am, he will use the transporter to come for me?'

'It's a she and I hoped that we could keep her occupied with the battle.' Bruno muttered petulantly.

Elzbieta gave a nervous laugh and added, 'It doesn't matter where I am. I'm glad I killed her son and I will face her and fight to the end.'

'We will all stand together and make sure that you will not have to face her alone.' Summer responded.

Bruno watched the girls as they displayed their courage and determination with immense pride. He nodded but said nothing. Nothing more was needed to be said.

After listening about their unity, Greg spoke with urgency, 'I hate to remind you lot but Harry wants to see you all straight away. He is waiting for you in the lab.'

'No point putting off the inevitable,' Bruno's voice trembled slightly. 'Come on you two, lets go,' He placed one arm around Summer and the other around Elzbieta. Turning to Charlie and Greg he said in a quiet tone, 'We will see you soon.'

Greg watched his friends go out the door and his heart sunk. He pondered whether he had done the right thing by not telling them how terrifying and painful the process would be. He then thought about the emotions he had at the time. Ignorance had been his friend. Even though he was anxious and scared, it would have been far worse if he had known the truth.

CHAPTER THIRTY ONE

THE TRANSPORTER ROOM

'IT ITCHES,' COMPLAINED Summer as she scratched her arm fiercely.

'Stop doing that, it's so irritating.' Elzbieta grumbled as she rubbed her own arm agitatedly.

Bruno sat quietly in Harry's office occupied with examining the palm of his hand where the weapon had been inserted. He could not believe what they had just been through and thought back to Greg's assurance that it would not be painful. The wailing of the machine as it messed with his brain was alarmingly and grated the insides of his head. The lotion was unbearably itchy and made his skin so hard and dry that he felt revolted every time he touched it.

All they were given was one day and now they had been called into Harry's office without any training whatsoever. The whole process was rushed and this worried Bruno immensely. At least Greg had two days including intensive training.

All three fell into an uncomfortable silence. Bruno remained seated whilst the girls paced the room. They all waited for Harry.

After a few moments, the door slid open and Harry entered. He looked very tired and the lines on his forehead were deeper. Worry and exhaustion were leaving their marks. The dark circles beneath his sunken eyes gave away sleepless nights.

'I have called you here as time is short. The Gwarks are aware that they can now use the transporter successfully. They could be here any time.' His voice was still firm and full of authority but his expression gave away how vulnerable he truly felt.

'Are you suggesting we go to their planet soon?' Bruno asked.

Harry looked at Bruno and replied quietly, 'Not soon, now.'

Bruno's eyes widened with astonishment and he gave Summer and Elzbieta a quick glance to see their reactions. They too, were wide eyed.

'We have not even learnt how to use the weapon yet. You put us through so much and they are useless to us without the training.' Bruno gabbled frantically.

Harry held up his hand to gain Bruno's complete attention. Bruno upon seeing this snapped his mouth shut.

'In order for the weapon to work well, you will have to take the pill and be like one of us. Greg was a special case as he is far more responsive due to the advanced nature of his brain.' Harry explained.

'Are you telling us that Greg is more intelligent than us?' Bruno gave a nervous laugh.

'In some ways, yes. He thinks differently to any of you.' Harry replied in a matter of fact way.

This frank reply shocked Bruno and he was unable to respond against it.

'You will take the pill soon after you land on Gwark soil and this will enable you use the laser gun. Trust me.' Harry continued, 'I need this to work as much as you do.'

Harry paused and turned his attention to Elzbieta. He walked towards her and placed his hand gently on her shoulder and said, 'Elzbieta, I would prefer it if you stayed here and fought with us. There is no doubt that the Gwarks will take full advantage of transporting themselves on Nimara. We need your help here.'

Elzbieta pressed her lips firmly together and shook her head adamantly, 'No way. I appreciate your concern and I know why you want me to stay here but I will stand my ground and fight as I should. My place is with my friends and obviously I am destined to fight the Gwark leader. I am not backing out.'

Harry pressed her shoulder and nodded. His face grew soft as he felt such pride in the young girl.

Bruno broke in, 'What about our soldiers?'

Harry turned to Bruno and smiled, 'They are already being fitted with the weapon and the lotion has been applied. I want them all to assemble outside the transporter room in half an hour. Greg is already outside the transporter room and is waiting for you. No time like the present, you will go first.'

Bruno could not believe how quickly everything was moving and barely had time to think before he found himself outside the dreaded door. He was pleased to see that Greg, who had waited for some time, was shuffling from one foot to the other and his hands tapped rhythmically by his sides. He was extremely nervous and this made Bruno feel better about himself.

They all entered the room and Bruno found himself once more surrounded by the colour cream. He could feel the carpet beneath his feet but could not gain any sense of where the walls or ceiling began. It was a strange and disorientating feeling.

Harry called out to them as he glided back towards the door, 'Good luck and remember, united you fight and united you will succeed.'

Then there was an eerie silence. Even though the room was so white it somehow began to blur and a sound like whooshing air was followed by the feeling of being sucked up into a black hole. Bruno, Summer, Elzbieta and Greg had disappeared.

CHAPTER THIRTY TWO

HERBERT TAKES CONTROL

THE WHOLE APARTMENT was unusually quiet and Herbert swished his tail back and forth with boredom. It took him back to the time when he first came to live there with Charlie and past many a day filled with silence. Back then he enjoyed the hours spent, sleeping, eating, listening to the ticking of the clock and watching passers-by from his window. Now solitude lost its appeal as he had grown accustomed to the clinking and clanking of dishes as Greg was being creative in the kitchen. He enjoyed the times when Greg would come into his room and spend time talking to him or stroking his head. In fact, even when they sat together in silence, the company was a comfort to him. He delighted in the giggles and chatter between the four friends, Bruno, Summer, Elzbieta and Greg when Charlie was busy at work. The humans were a constant source of entertainment to him and he grew to like them very much.

Now, life returned back to how it was during the days when he spent the time on his own. He moaned to himself softly, feeling very sorry for himself. Then suddenly as he was about to close his eyes and have a snooze, he heard a loud crash coming from one of the rooms down the corridor. This was quickly followed by a heavy thump. Herbert flicked his eyes wide open and smoke smouldered from his nostrils like an active volcano ready to erupt. He edged towards the door but felt the chain around his collar holding him back. It never bothered him before but at this very moment he needed to set himself free of it. He forced his neck against the chain but it would not move. Turning around to have a better look at it, he could see that it was thick and solid but luckily for him it was made of metal. Herbert breathed in deeply and opened his mouth wide and bellowed out scorching hot fire. Part of the chain turned white with the heat and the dragon quickly bit the weak part and it snapped.

Herbert dashed out of the room together with the remaining piece of chain attached to his collar flapping in the air. Another bang alerted him that the noise was coming from the lounge. Without hesitation, he galloped straight through the door and was astonished to see three hog like aliens swinging large hammers and destroying everything in the room. This was his master's pride and joy and these trespassers were ruining the table, chairs, settee and even trying to knock down the walls. Filled with rage, the dragon raised himself up on his hind legs and roared loudly. The Gwarks stared at the dragon dumbfounded. Before any of them could move, Herbert opened his mouth once more and a torrent of red hot flames gushed out. As soon as they touched them, the Gwarks disintegrated into small piles of dust. Satisfied, Herbert waddled over to the piles of dust and with a swift movement of his tail, brushed them away until they were no longer in sight.

He remembered that the same kind of creature recently appeared in his room and began to worry that Charlie could be in danger. He could not understand why anyone could possibly hate Charlie but it was clear to him that these aliens were no friends of his. Herbert began to panic and decided that he must find Charlie to protect him from the creatures. He moved towards the locked window and knew that the only way out was to smash through it. He stood as far back from the window as he could and then with a loud roar ran towards the window with all his might smashing the glass and then flying up to the open sky, spreading his large wings, pumping them up and down until he was soaring high above the ground. Herbert never ventured far from the building before because when Charlie took off his collar and watched him as he swooped and dived, enjoying the exercise, he liked to remain in his master's vision. This was a completely new experience for him. He had no idea where Charlie worked, therefore, he would have to rely on sniffing out the delicate scent of his master. As he flew, the scent became stronger and it was not long before he was above the building where Charlie was working on transporting the soldiers to the planet of the Gwarks.

Herbert landed at the front gates and waddled into the building. He went down many corridors and passed many rooms. He was met with surprised faces but no-one even tried to stop him.

Finally, he stood outside the room where Charlie was. Using his snout to open the door, he took a peek inside and saw his master pushing buttons and concentrating on another room behind a huge glass window. As Herbert looked through it, he could see a few Nimarans standing nervously inside before they vanished. This did not interest him very much as he was overjoyed to see that Charlie was safe.

Charlie stopped working the controls and slowly turned around as though he sensed he was being watched. As soon as his eyes settled on Herbert, who was now sitting back on his hind legs with his plump bottom spread like a thick cushion on the floor and grinning with his tongue poking out of the side of his open mouth, Charlie looked at him questioningly and said, 'Herbert, what are you doing here? How did you get out of the apartment? Get in quickly before anyone sees you. Harry would kill me if he knew you were here.' Charlie berated the dragon as he attempted to pull him into the room. Once the dragon was across the threshold, Charlie closed the door. 'Why did you come here, for goodness sake?'

The dragon tried to communicate that he wanted to protect his master by curling his tail around him. This made Charlie smile but he misunderstood what the dragon meant, 'Ah I see, you missed me.' He giggled. 'Look, just sit by the wall and be quiet. I have a lot of work to do right now.'

Disgruntled the dragon obeyed and waddled towards the wall. He circled round three times before settling down and watched Charlie return to the buttons as more Nimarans entered the room beyond the window.

Just as Charlie was about to press one of the buttons, five Gwarks suddenly appeared less than two feet behind him. Herbert leapt up and instantly swung his tail like a whip and pushed Charlie to the side. With one fiery breath the Gwarks became dust. Shocked, Charlie watched as Herbert moved towards the pile of dust and swished his tail around until it all disappeared. Satisfied, the dragon returned to his place by the wall.

'You knew they were going to come here,' Charlie uttered in disbelief and admiration. Realising he had left his duty, he quickly returned to the desk and frantically began pressing the buttons until the next group of Nimarans were transported.

'I got to tell Harry about this. Everyone needs to be warned. The Gwarks could land at any time and anywhere on our planet. Thank goodness Harry insisted that Rose should stay here and not in her cottage alone.'

Charlie quickly faced the screen on the desk and waved his hand in front of it. Straight away the black screen became white and Harry's face appeared.

'Charlie, what is the matter?' Harry asked instantly. Obviously, Harry was waiting for any update on the process of transporting the soldiers to the Gwarks planet.

'The Gwarks have started to land. We must send out a warning to the rest of the people. They must be armed and ready and stay in groups,' Charlie explained.

'I knew they would be quick. Leave it with me, I will warn everyone.' After he finished speaking screen went blank and darkened once more.

Charlie sighed and turned to the dragon, 'I hope everything is going okay for Bruno and the others on the Gwark planet.' He approached the dragon who bowed his head ready to be stroked. Charlie almost placed his hand on Herbert's head but changed his mind. Smiling proudly, he shook his head and wrapped his arms around the dragon's neck. In response, the dragon curled his tail around his master protectively and lovingly.

CHAPTER THIRTY THREE

A HOSTILE ENVIRONMENT

THE DARK SKY was thick with smog and as Bruno inhaled, the taste of soot coated his tongue and filled his nostrils like tar. Each time he breathed in, it caused him to choke as the dirt grated his throat. He looked at Summer and Elzbieta and noticed that their beautiful soft blonde hair had already been coated with the dust and grime making the various golden tones dull and dark. The lively way that their hair swished around as they moved now lay flat and in clumps, matted down like a heavy scarf.

The sky was a block of black, cloudless, void of any stars and not even one moon beamed down. Looking around, Bruno noticed that the whole area around him was flat and empty. There were no trees, bushes, flowers, rocks or hills; the whole environment was hostile. Bruno also became aware that there was an absence of wind. The whole atmosphere was stifling.

The four of them remained where they were and waited for the soldiers to appear. Summer touched the ground which was covered with the same soot and dust that smothered the air. It was cold to the touch, sharp and left lines of dirt on her hand. Casually she wiped the hand on her trousers. Elzbieta scoured the area to see if there was anything more than just barren land. Turning slowly she scanned the entire area and then spotted something in the distance. She pointed to the others who turned to face the direction that she was referring to. There were blocks of concrete and steel which could only suggest a city of some sort. Even from this distance, it looked plain and dirty. Suddenly there was a whistle and ten soldiers popped up from nowhere. Once they materialised, they also looked around at the surroundings. Bruno realised that none of the Nimaran people had ever visited this planet before and were just as curious as they were. After the first soldiers arrived the others followed very quickly until they were all united and ready for battle.

Greg who was standing silently up to now asked, 'Where is Charlie?' as he was trying to find him in the crowd.

One of the soldiers stepped towards him and replied, 'Charlie is required on Nimara, he is in charge of transportation. Harry felt that he would be more useful there.'

Greg nodded and was relieved to hear that for the moment he was safe from the danger they now faced.

'I'm here,' a small voice was heard from within the crowd. Stepping forward was Tim; he looked so small between the other Nimarans who towered above him. Bruno smiled down at Tim, amused at how small he was compared to the other aliens.

'Charlie transported you here?' Bruno asked confused. Charlie always wanted to protect his little friend from danger as much as possible.

'He did not notice me sneak in and stand between the rest of the soldiers.' Tim replied. 'I want to fight for Nimara and its people.'

'Well, you are here now so just be careful. Stick with me. I got to make sure that you get back home in one piece,' Bruno ordered. He was very aware of how much suffering Charlie had gone through, he did not deserve to lose anyone else, especially his best friend.

'So, what now?' Summer enquired.

Bruno thought for a moment and then in a firm, confident voice replied, pointing at the same time, 'We will walk to the city over there. Hopefully we can easily gain entry and take them by surprise. The Gwarks are too sure of themselves and probably do not expect us to take the initiative. They believe that we would be too scared to step on their planet. This could be to our advantage.'

The soldiers formed various sized groups and led by the humans, began to walk towards the central city that they could see in the distance.

They all walked in silence, each concentrating on breathing through the thick, hot air. All of them were frightened. They had won the battle previously but that was on familiar territory. This time they had ventured into the unknown with weapons that they had not even practiced with.

With each step the city became more and more visible. It consisted of many square buildings made from a dark grey stone. There were no windows in any of them just brick upon brick, all of equal size and shape.

The land looked the same as where they landed, flat and without any vegetation. There were no birds in the sky or animals lurking around. The only sound was the thud of heavy machinery. The monotonous thud, thud, thud became irritating.

When the soldiers had reached the gates of the city, they stood against the high wall and waited for their orders. They all looked at Bruno who was trying to peer through a small gap in the gate to get some sense of what was going on inside.

'Bruno,' Greg tapped him on the shoulder, 'Why don't we just go for it and crash through?'

Bruno turned and faced Greg, 'We have to be very careful. We must not alert them of our arrival before we are in a strong position.'

Bruno turned his attention back to the gap.

'But we are in a strong position now. Our weapons are extremely powerful. All of us blasting off the lasers simultaneously will be enough of a surprise. We could descend on them within moments and don't forget the lotion will protect us. How much stronger could we be?' Greg argued firmly. 'By stalling, we could be seen and ruin the element of surprise.'

Bruno looked at Summer and Elzbieta who were listening intently to the conversation. They nodded in agreement with Greg.

'Ok, firstly we tell the soldiers that we will storm the place. Everyone will aim their lasers at the gate and then continue to fire until we get inside. From then on we will all have to rely on our instincts I'm afraid. We will just have to hope that the lotion works for all of us.' Bruno decided, 'Then we take the pill.'

'I will not need to.' Greg interjected.

'We know that Greg but we do.' Summer smiled gently at him.

All four of them went together to give orders to the soldiers who in turn were ready to obey every command. It never ceased to amaze the humans how much trust they put in them. After this the friends, quickly returned to the gates. Tim kept himself close to Bruno's side. Bruno took out a small box that contained many pills and distributed one each to Summer and Elzbieta. Greg merely watched as they swallowed the pill at the same time. Instantly after taking it, the changes started to occur. Their whole bodies began to quiver and lose its original shape and individual molecules broke away from the mass and circled around as if finding a new place to settle. The overall effect was like bees around honey comb, all fighting to land in a good place. Within seconds their new shape was formed and there was no distinction in their appearance with that of the Nimaran aliens. For a moment they stared at each other and then the weapon in their palms buzzed. It was now connected to their new brain patterns formed by the transformation.

'Bruno now spoke in a strange, quivery voice not unlike that of the aliens and said, 'We are ready.'

With this, Greg and the newly formed aliens stepped away from the gates. Seeing this all of the Nimaran aliens did the same.

Bruno cried out, 'Three… two… one… fire!'

All of the soldiers blasted an array of coloured lasers at the gate and surrounding wall. Within seconds the whole area disintegrated and they charged forward continuing to shoot light beams from their palms. They had entered the city and straight away were faced with the astonished faces of the Gwarks. A siren was sounded and more and more Gwarks spilled out from the buildings into the square paving area in the centre of the city. They were armed with axes and laser guns. However, every shot they fired had no effect when it made contact with a Nimaran body.

Bruno realised that they were invincible. It would be impossible to lose the fight.

As each row of Gwarks moved forward, the Nimaran soldiers simply blasted them away. The moment the laser reached the Gwarks, they disintegrated. After four rows had been exterminated, the Gwarks ceased coming forwards. Some of them began to look around to see what the others were doing. A few began to take steps back and the some of the others seeing this, followed their example. Several of them even dropped their weapons and run as fast as they could to safety. The Gwarks were clearly in complete chaos and confusion.

The Nimarans could not believe how quickly the Gwarks gave up the fight. They had expected them to be far more resilient than that. Suddenly a loud cry came from one of the high buildings. Everyone looked up to see the Commander standing in full view, her arms spread out high above her head which was thrown back. Her shrill scream was long and piercing. She was furious. The Nimaran soldiers bared their long, pointed teeth at her. The Gwarks had stopped running and trembled with fear. Bruno could not believe that these strong, ghastly creatures were afraid of a female. What had happened to them since they fought two years previously? They were barely recognisable as the warriors that caused everyone in the solar system to quake at the mere thought of them.

'Cowards! Fools! Idiots!' she bellowed harshly at her men. 'How dare you run away from those pathetic maggots. Fight... fight to the death... FIGHT!' the commander roared shaking her fists in the air.

The Gwarks however, bowed their heads and remained in their places.

Out of control and absolutely bubbling over with anger, the Commander looked at the Nimaran side, 'Where is that disgusting girl called Elzbieta. I know she is there hiding amongst you.' She spat venomously.

Bruno gently pushed Elzbieta back a bit and shook his head. However, Elzbieta was not going to back down from a fight, not when they got this far. Slowly she walked to the front of the line and as loudly as she could shout, 'I am here. I think we have some unfinished business, is that right?'

'Ah! I see you have taken alien form again. Not strong enough as a human are you?' the commander growled. She flung herself off the ledge that she was standing on and landed in a crouching position on the ground before Elzbieta. Even though she was frightened, Elzbieta could not help but to be impressed by the woman's agility.

The Commander stood up and walked over to Elzbieta. Her mammoth size was intimidating but Elzbieta did not even blink. She remained rooted to the spot by sheer determination. This was going to be her fight and she would win.

The Commander raised her arm high and swung it down meaning to strike the girl in the face. Her long talons ready to slice into her skin and rip it open. Elzbieta jumped to the side and could feel those pointed nails run through her hair. The Commander lunged forward once more but Elzbieta ducked and dived to prevent being hurt by the crazy woman.

'Remember the lotion! Don't be afraid,' Greg called out and Elzbieta turned round to see who had said that. Due to the distraction, the commander attacked once more and tried to dig her nails into Elzbieta's stomach. All Elzbieta felt was a slight press of four nails but nothing more. The Commander however, was wailing in pain and held her hand before her eyes in disbelief. All four of her nails had broken and the tips of her fingers were bleeding. The force of hitting the hardened stomach had snapped her nails off and broke her fingers.

Elzbieta pushed the palm of her hand forward to face in the direction of the Commander and let the laser shoot out. Not taking proper aim, the laser sliced through the Commanders arm. It cut the arm off at the elbow and scorching the skin, sealed the wound. The commander opened her snout so wide that it looked ready to split in half and ensued with an earth shattering scream. She fell to the floor writhing in agony as everyone else merely watched. None of the Gwarks moved to help her. They were all spellbound by what they had just witnessed.

Elzbieta stepped towards the Commander and shouted, 'Give up?'

'Never,' replying with great difficulty from utter pain.

Elzbieta screamed out once more, 'Give up?'

Tears were rolling down her hog-like face, her excruciating pain was clear and yet she repeated, 'Never.'

Elzbieta knelt down beside the Commander and with a soft and calm voice said, 'I am not afraid of you. You have lost. Give up.'

The Commander began to cry freely and cradled the stump with her other hand.

Elzbieta could no longer bear to watch this and turned to find Bruno, who was staring open mouthed at what was going on.

'Bruno, the serum. Have you got it?' she shouted.

Bruno shook his head but Greg answered, 'I have got it. Here, catch.' He flung the bottle high in the air. His aim was perfect. Elzbieta raised her hand and caught it. Quickly opening the bottle, she whispered to the Commander saying, 'A token of our good will. Never bother us again and we will never bother you.'

She tipped the bottle over the stump and three droplets fell onto it. The raw wound turned pink and the bone began to grow and once it reached the right length formed a skeleton hand. The Commander could now move each digit. Then the muscles began to form around the white bone and the sinews appeared. Everyone gasped as this happened. Finally, the skin coated the flesh and the hairs grew back. Even the talons grew back but they were no longer a deep red instead a pale shade of yellow. Elzbieta was amused to think that the Gwark would have to use nail varnish.

Astonished, the Commander moved her arm around and wiggled her fingers. She stood up and turned to her army. She was about to give them orders but each one of them threw down their weapons and looked at the ground. They had no fight left in them.

Loosing the power and respect of her army she turned back to Elzbieta and said vehemently, 'You have not heard the last of me. I will get you in the end. Mark my words.' Just as she said this her head split in two and blood splattered across Elzbieta's shocked face. The Commander fell to the floor and was dead before she even touched the ground. A Gwark stood looking down at the dead body, holding an axe in his hand dripping with blood. Breathing heavily, looked at Elzbieta, then lowering the axe moved back to his place.

'Since our last battle and the death of her son, she has ruled with oppression, corruption and bloody rage. We were all waiting for the right moment to be rid of her and this was the right time,' he explained in a husky growl.

Bruno stepped forward to greet the Gwark and said, 'Perhaps one day you could live in peace with the Nimarans.'

'Peace with the Nimarans? Never.' Then turning towards the Nimaran aliens he continued by saying. 'We will always despise you and your soft ways. Now go while you can.' After this, the Gwark raised his hand in the air and all the other Gwarks began to turn and walk back to their buildings.

'Wait! There is one more thing.' Bruno called out.

The Gwark stopped and turned around to face him.

'You have one of the Nimarans held prisoner. We want him back.' Bruno demanded.

The Gwark frowned, 'He betrayed his people and yet they want him back? This is one reason that we will never understand you people. Fine, have him. He has no use to us now. Give me a simple axe and I know how to use it.' He raised his hand in the air once more and all the Gwarks went into the buildings.

Bruno watched as they went inside, leaving them to stand alone in the square and leaving the Commander to rot.

Moments later a small Nimaran stumbled out of the building. His hands and feet were still shackled and tears streamed down his hollow cheeks.

As soon as he was near to his people he fell to the ground. Some of the soldiers ran forward and lifted him up. Whispering words of comfort, they gently poured water into his mouth and attempted to bandage his many wounds.

Bruno regarded this and could not believe how relentless these people's compassion and forgiveness was. No, the Gwarks could never understand them and in many ways neither could he.

'Tim, how do we get back?' Bruno panicked.

'No problem, I took liberty of snatching this before I left.' He showed Bruno a thick, leather like device that was firmly wrapped around his wrist. 'Once pressed, it will signal Charlie to transport us back immediately.' Without another word he pressed a tiny button in the centre of the device and they all disappeared into thin air.

CHAPTER THIRTY FOUR

BACK TO NIMARA

THE BRIGHTNESS OF the room made Bruno's eyes water and he winced in pain. Slowly, as his eyes grew accustomed to the light, he could see that Summer, Elzbieta, Greg and Tim were with him and therefore, arrived safely back to Nimara. They were the last ones to leave the Gwark planet. As he looked at his friends, he could see that they had returned to their natural form. Staring down at his own body, he too, was back to normal. What amazed him the most was that that he did not feel a thing. The pill must have been perfected to Bruno's relief.

All the Nimarans had already gone to be united with there loved ones and bursting to share their adventure with them.

Charlie entered the room and ran straight up to Tim. He looked angrily at his friend and seeing that he was perfectly alright, grabbed him and held him tightly. No words were needed, he was just glad to see that his friend had returned safely.

Harry stood at the door and his presence dominated the room. Even though he looked worn out with dark lines under his eyes, he still was a magnificent enigma. Bruno bowed slightly to acknowledge him.

Harry seemed to ignore this and was purely focussed on his friend and immediately spoke to him, 'Simon, my friend, you are home.'

Simon stepped forward and all the emotions of fear and pain burst out of him through a flood of tears, 'Forgive this fool,' he choked.

'Forgiveness has already been given,' Harry held out his hand to Simon. 'We need to take care of you now.'

Simon lowered his head in shame but took Harry's hand in his.

Harry smiled gently and then nodded to two of the soldiers who lingered in the doorway. Immediately they both moved either side of Simon and gently took him under the arms and led him out of the room to the medical room where he could be attended to.

Once Simon was out of the room, Harry turned his attention towards the four humans. His whole demeanour changed and his relief was clear. 'It seems that your adventure was a success and the battle was easily won.'

'Yes,' Bruno replied, 'All due to the weapons and the lotion. There was no way the Gwarks could harm us.'

Harry nodded proudly at this, 'Thank you for bringing Simon back home.'

'Talking of home, when are we going back?' Greg asked eagerly.

Harry turned to Greg and patted him on the head adoringly, 'Of course you want to return home but first the doctors will remove your weapons and the serum will heal your hands straight away. Do not worry, the procedure is completely painless and you will be put to sleep when we take the weapon out. Then, you can go straight away.'

'How do you know that the serum works, you were not with us on the planet when I used it on the Commander?' Elzbieta questioned.

Harry smiled and replied, 'The soldiers arrived before you and told me all about it. They have great admiration for you Elzbieta. That was a brave fight.' Harry made Elzbieta blush. 'Come, let's get you to the laboratory.'

Bruno stepped forward and placed his hand on Harry's arm, 'Wait. There is something I would like to do before we go home.'

Harry looked closely at Bruno and then with a gentle voice said, 'Oh, of course. I imagine you will want to visit a certain place. Let's sort your hand out and then you will have as much time as you need.

CHAPTER THIRTY FIVE

HOME

BRUNO ENTERED THE chapel and like the previous time was filled with awe at the beauty of the place. The atmosphere was calming and Bruno felt quite relaxed. His attention turned to the statue that stood on a wooden table in the corner of the room. It was still as magnificent as when he saw it the first time. Bruno gently touched the fingers of the statue of Granddad once more and looked up at the kind face.

'I hope that you are proud of me.' He spoke to Granddad. 'We won the battle again.' He paused to swallow the lump that was caught in his throat.

He looked around at the beautiful stained glass and how the light created coloured beams across the room. This place was truly mesmerising and Bruno felt it was the most perfect place for a memorial for Granddad to be.

'I hope that we will meet again in my dreams.' After saying this, he kissed his own fingers and touched them on the statue's hand. 'I am now ready to go home.'

Slowly, Bruno walked out of the chapel and stopped at the door. He looked back at the statue and gave a melancholic smile. He did not know if he would ever return to this place again. His work was done.

As he approached the door to the transporter room, he saw his friends waiting or him. They were obviously eager to get going. Quickening his pace, he sprinted over to them and they went inside together.

Harry and Charlie were already inside. Herbert was coiled around his master and jumped up excitedly when he saw the humans arrive. 'Herbert wanted to say good bye.' Charlie sniffled. His eyes were red from the tears that he shed. 'I hate good byes.' He gave as an excuse for his emotional state.

'Is this really it? Are we really saying goodbye or do you think we will see each other again?' Summer asked.

'Who knows,' Harry answered. 'We do not know what the future will bring. I just hope if we do ever meet again, it will be in happier circumstances.'

'We will never forget you.' Greg whimpered, clearly upset.

'Of course, we will never forget you and what you have done for us again.' Harry returned. 'No use in stalling. May your futures be bright.' For a moment he remained still and just stared at the four friends as if trying to capture that moment which could be the last one that they would ever have together.

Then, he motioned for them to enter the room.

Charlie suddenly rushed up to Bruno and hugged him tightly, 'I will deeply miss you my friend.' He loosened his grip and turned to the others, 'I will miss you all.' Then he swiftly made his way out of the transporter room.

All four of them stood in the room when suddenly the light dazzled them once more. Just as their eyes started to grow accustomed to the light… they disappeared.

★

'Mum is always snowed under mountains of paperwork these days.' Summer said eagerly.

'Now, I think it's time for Bruno to open up his presents!' Bruno's father interrupted.

These words were a blur and a sound like whooshing air was followed by the feeling of being sucked up into a black hole.

Without hesitation Bruno began to tear off the wrapping paper and was just about to see what was inside. Suddenly he stopped, realising that he was actually back home. He looked at the excited faces of his parents who were none the wiser that he had ever left. He turned to look at Summer and Elzbieta who also seemed to be slightly disorientated by the whole situation. Returning to his present, Bruno ripped off the remaining paper and opened the box and inside it was a model of a laser gun.

He looked at his parents who were skipping with joy. The present was expensive but Bruno begged them to buy it for him some time ago. He returned his attention to his present. After experiencing a real laser gun, the one in the box lost its appeal. When he pressed the button it made a buzzing noise and a little light flashed at the end of the nozzle. Even Summer and Elzbieta looked disappointed.

Forcing a smile he tried to appear as enthusiastic as possible, 'Oh Mum, Dad, this is just perfect. Thank you.'

Bruno realised that it was going to be very difficult to adapt to his world once again.

Lightning Source UK Ltd.
Milton Keynes UK
UKOW02f2223300415

250698UK00001B/5/P